Kitten Kaboodle

by

Kathi Daley

I want to thank the very talented Jessica Fischer for the cover art.

I so appreciate Bruce Curran, who is always ready and willing to answer my cyber questions.

And, of course, thanks to the readers and bloggers in my life, who make doing what I do possible.

Thank you to Randy Ladenheim-Gil for the editing.

Special thanks to Joanne Kocourek, Donna Walo-Clancy, Vivian Shane, and Nancy Farris for submitting recipes.

And finally I want to thank my sister Christy for always lending an ear and my husband Ken for allowing me time to write by taking care of everything else.

Books by Kathi Daley

Come for the murder, stay for the romance.

Zoe Donovan Cozy Mystery:

Halloween Hijinks
The Trouble With Turkeys
Christmas Crazy
Cupid's Curse
Big Bunny Bump-off
Beach Blanket Barbie
Maui Madness
Derby Divas
Haunted Hamlet
Turkeys, Tuxes, and Tabbies
Christmas Cozy
Alaskan Alliance
Matrimony Meltdown
Soul Surrender
Heavenly Honeymoon
Hopscotch Homicide
Ghostly Graveyard
Santa Sleuth
Shamrock Shenanigans
Kitten Kaboodle

Whales and Tails Cozy Mystery:

Romeow and Juliet
The Mad Catter
Grimm's Furry Tail
Much Ado About Felines
Legend of Tabby Hollow
Cat of Christmas Past
A Tale of Two Tabbies
The Great Catsby – *July 2016*

Seacliff High Mystery:

The Secret
The Curse
The Relic
The Conspiracy
The Grudge

Sand and Sea Hawaiian Mystery:

Murder at Dolphin Bay
Murder at Sunrise Beach – *June 2016*

Road to Christmas Romance:

Road to Christmas Past

Chapter 1

Monday, August 8

I'd like to think that the line between right and wrong is clearly defined, but the reality is, there are times in our lives when the only real choice lies in the gray space between what society tells us we *should* do and what you know in your heart you *must* do. My own journey into the gray space began when my husband Zak Zimmerman's honorary grandmother came to town. Technically, Nona isn't related to Zak, but the Harley-riding senior citizen has ensconced herself into the family in such a way that there isn't a Zimmerman alive who doesn't either love or fear her. The most important thing to know about Nona is that she's not only a strong and opinionated woman who's willing to fight for what she believes but she's just a tiny bit crazy as well.

I first had the opportunity to meet Nona the previous summer, when she came to stay with us for Zak and my wedding. I wasn't sure what to make of the uninhibited woman who insisted on practicing nude yoga on the beach until she whisked me away on her pink motorcycle and helped me solve the murder that had been weighing on my mind. Nona and I had a grand adventure that earned her a permanent place in my heart. Prior to returning home after the wedding, she'd promised to come back for an extended visit, and if there was one thing you could say for Nona it's that she kept her promises. Unfortunately, it was in keeping this promise that she happened to meet a kindergarten teacher and animal activist named Aspen Woods, who was embroiled in a battle with a kitten mill owner named Edna Leech, and the controversy that would touch all our lives was born.

"Zoe Donovan, have you heard a word I've said?" my best friend Ellie Davis asked. Ellie had just returned from a month-long visit with her mother and we were having a girls' night out. We used to hang out almost every day, but our one-on-one time had become a rare thing since I'd become both a wife and a surrogate mother to three minors.

"I'm listening. You were talking about the new dress you picked up on your vacation."

"Twenty minutes and three subjects ago."

"I'm sorry. I guess I'm a little distracted. What is it we were talking about?"

"Dentures."

I frowned.

"My Great-Aunt Clarissa called me early this morning to complain that one of the men at the assisted living facility we moved her into had stolen her dentures. When I tried to explain that was highly unlikely because dentures were made to fit a person's mouth and the man she was accusing was a great, big man and she was a teeny, tiny woman, she informed me that the man didn't steal them for himself but for his new girlfriend, who'd recently moved into the adjoining room and, having lost all her teeth, couldn't eat anything harder than Jell-O."

"I assume there's more to this story?"

"Of course there's more to the story. I haven't even gotten to the part about the Pomeranian with the head cold yet."

Pomeranian with a head cold? "I'm sorry, go on."

"Anyway, as I was saying, after I hung up with Aunt Clarissa I called the man who runs the place and told him about the dentures. Now, keep in mind that Aunt

Clarissa has become more than just a little forgetful in the past few years, so we both assumed she'd simply misplaced her teeth the way she misplaced her going-out-to-supper wig a few weeks ago."

"You mean the pink one?"

"No. The pink one is her company's-coming-to-visit wig; the blue one is the wig of choice for outings away from the home. Anyway, as I was saying, we just assumed Clarissa misplaced the dentures, so we decided to ..."

I guess I must have zoned out again because the next thing I knew, Ellie was staring at me with a huge grin and a look of expectation on her face. "So what do you think?"

"Think?"

Ellie groaned. "Okay, that was the funniest story I've ever told in my entire life and you weren't even listening. What's on your mind that has you so distracted?"

"Kittens."

"Kittens?"

I looked around the restaurant to see who might be listening in on our conversation, but apparently not a single soul was interested in Ellie's long, drawn-out story about her Aunt Clarissa. "I have six stolen kittens hidden in my guest room."

"You stole kittens?"

"I didn't steal the kittens, but I'm pretty sure I know who did."

"Who?"

I leaned in close and lowered my voice. Not that anyone would care about a boxful of kittens. "Do you remember Nona?"

"Zak's crazy relative with the pink Harley who almost got you killed last summer?"

"That's the one. Shortly after you left to visit your mother, she showed up on her Harley and announced she was staying with us for the rest of the summer. Of course I was delighted to have her because, unlike the rest of Zak's relatives, real or honorary, Nona is a Zimmerman affiliate I actually like. Anyway, a few days after she arrived she introduced me to a new friend she'd met at the yoga class she'd signed up for. The friend, whose name is Aspen Woods, is a lovely woman around our age who's been on a campaign to shut down a kitten mill she'd discovered outside of town. Nona figured that because I owned and operated a wild and domestic animal rescue and rehabilitation shelter maybe I could help Aspen accomplish what she'd been unable to on her own."

"And did you? Help her?"

"I tried, but in the end I didn't meet with much success. Aspen had already filed a complaint with the county, but the county determined that the cats weren't being abused. Although they're in pens and unable to roam free, at the time of the inspection they were mostly healthy and well fed. The pens were clean, and due to their size, the fact that they were locked up wasn't considered cruel. Aspen insisted that when she visited the property there were both adult cats as well as kittens that were clearly sick, but the county animal control didn't find sick animals at the time of their inspection, so it was determined there was nothing they could do. I tried to argue that the property owner knew of the inspection and would have simply moved any sick animals, but in the end I was told to butt out and stop harassing the woman."

"And did you?"

"Mostly, for the sake of the Zoo. I need to play nice with the county so the operating agreement between the Zoo and the county isn't suspended. I hate to say it, but I'm really at their mercy." I paused as a wave of uncertainty washed over me. There was a time when I would have leaped into the fray without a second thought, but the responsibility of owning a business and being a wife and surrogate mother had changed the way I interacted with people in my personal life. There were times, such as now, when I wasn't sure how I really felt about the changes I'd made. Don't get me wrong: I love my family and I love my life. but when I look at Nona and her devil-may-care attitude, there are times I miss the old, spontaneous Zoe.

"I've been helping, though," I continued. "In a politically correct sort of way. I've been quietly meeting with a couple of members of the town council on a plan to change our local laws to better define what is and isn't an abusive environment. The problem is that even if I am successful in getting new legislation approved, it will take months or even years to really make a difference. Besides the time lag, there's also the fact that the county would have to adopt the town's legislation for it to be enforced outside the town limits."

"So even if you're successful it most likely won't do much to help the current situation."

"Exactly. Aspen and Nona, however, aren't dependent on the goodwill of the county and are on a mission to save the cats no matter what. When it became apparent that the county was unwilling to do anything, Aspen began picketing the county offices and Nona began engaging in public displays of verbal abuse."

Ellie laughed. "Verbal abuse?"

"You know Nona. She's a feisty sort who isn't afraid to tell it like it is. She's got a razor-sharp tongue and she manages to draw quite a bit of attention."

"Is it working? The verbal abuse and the picketing?"

"Unfortunately, no. The harder Aspen and Nona try to get the place shut down, the more the property owner, Edna Leech, digs in her heels, and the county has all but washed their hands of the whole thing."

"Okay, I have an overview of the situation, but what does this have to do with the kittens in your guest room?" Ellie prompted.

I took a sip of my water before I continued. Several parties had come in since Ellie and I had begun our conversation, and I knew it wouldn't be long before our isolated table in the corner wasn't going to be quite so isolated. I lowered my voice just a bit for good measure. "Nona informed me this morning that she'd snuck onto Edna's property to check on the cats and she'd noticed a litter of kittens that appeared to be sick. She said she marched herself up to the house to demand that Edna obtain medical care for the kittens, but instead of agreeing, Edna told Nona that if she trespassed on her land again she would have her arrested; then she slammed the door in her face. Nona asked me if I could use my pull with the sheriff to investigate the matter, but Salinger was out of his office when I called, so I was unable to speak to him. Several hours later I found a box with six kittens on my front porch."

"If Nona is staying with you and she stole the cats, why wouldn't she just bring them inside?"

"I'm not sure unless she wanted me to honestly be able to say I didn't know where the kittens came from. I'm sure Nona doesn't want to get either of us in trouble, but it's clear the kittens need medical attention. I called Scott Walden," I said, referring to the local veterinarian, "and he came by to look at the babies. He confirmed that they're both ill and malnourished and gave me medicine and food supplements to help them get back to where they need to be."

Ellie sat back in her chair. She appeared to be contemplative, but I could tell she was concerned that I was harboring stolen kittens. Once she began to speak I knew I was right. "I know you're upset about the situation, and I agree the kitten mill needs to be shut down, but you have to take the kittens back. You know it's the right thing to do. Those kittens are worth a lot of money. Stealing, even for a good reason, is against the law. You could go to jail."

"I won't go to jail."

"You can't know that. If the cat woman presses charges Salinger might have no choice but to arrest you for possession of stolen property or harboring a criminal or something."

Ellie might be right, but Zoe Donovan the newly responsible woman had come to the end of her rope and Zoe Donovan the impulsive activist was about to take her place.

"I'm not taking the kittens back. I know it might be the legal thing to do, but there comes a time when you have to ignore what you *should* do in favor of what you *must* do."

"You know Salinger is going to realize you have the kittens as soon as this Edna Leech reports the theft."

I frowned. "I know that, and I'm willing to accept whatever consequences come my way. The strange thing is that I really expected Salinger to show up on my doorstep before this. Edna must realize the kittens are missing by now and she has to know it was Nona, Aspen, or me who took them. The fact that she hasn't reported the missing kittens seems a bit odd."

"I suppose she might realize that by bringing attention to the sick kittens it could endanger her entire operation. She might just let the whole thing go."

"Honestly, that's what I'm hoping, but letting it go doesn't seem like an Edna thing to do."

The hostess came by, causing a pause in our conversation as she sat the table next to us. After she left I decided it might be best to change the subject before someone overheard us and I asked Ellie about her visit to her mother.

"It was nice. When she told me she was going to sell the restaurant and move in with her best friend I thought it was a mistake, but she seems really happy. She's even made some new friends."

"That's awesome. I'm glad things worked out. It's been a little odd not finding your mom in the kitchen at Rosie's, but she's worked really hard and deserves a break."

"Yeah, I'm happy for her too, although I do really miss her. I think she's going to come for a visit in the fall. She wants to meet Brady."

"Speaking of Brady, how are things going between the two of you?"

"Fine," Ellie answered vaguely.

I knew Ellie's relationship with the new math teacher at Zimmerman Academy was complicated at best. Brady had moved to Ashton Falls just before Valentine's Day to replace Will Danner, the previous math teacher, who'd quit suddenly after he was offered a job that would allow him to be close to his elderly father. Zak and I had been out of town when Brady arrived with his four-year-old daughter, Holly, and twin eighteen-month-old sons, Haden and Hudson, so Ellie had volunteered to pick them up at the airport. Ellie had recently broken up with the love of her life, Levi Denton, and Brady had lost his wife to pneumonia fourteen months earlier. The two wounded souls seemed to have forged a bond that was, so far, more than a friendship but not quite a romance.

"Look, you know I hate to be nosy."

Ellie just looked at me.

"Okay, I quite enjoy being nosy. In fact, when it comes to people I love, I consider being nosy my job. The thing is that when I got home from Ireland it seemed obvious that you and Brady were working on building a relationship that was more than just fine. Over the next several months I witnessed the two of you spend a lot of time together even though you both insisted you were just friends, and then out of the blue you announced you were going to visit your mother, and would be gone for a month. It really doesn't take a genius to figure out that something must have occurred that would cause you to flee. My guess is that something has to do with Brady."

Ellie didn't answer, but I knew I was right.

"Look, we don't have to talk about this right now, but you know I'm here for you. We've been through a lot together during the course of our friendship. I don't know what's going on, but I do know you can talk to me about it."

"I know." Ellie smiled a weak sort of smile. "But not now and not here. Let's change the subject."

"Okay. What do you want to talk about?"

"Why don't you fill me in on what's going on with the Ashton Falls Event Committee? I know we have a meeting tomorrow and after being away for a month I feel totally out of the loop."

I shrugged. "Okay, if you really want to discuss the committee I'm game, but it's going to be a pretty boring conversation."

"At this moment, given our surroundings, I think boring is the most appropriate."

"Okay, if you say so. Let's see. There was a discussion at last week's meeting about doing a wine tasting toward the end of September. There was concern among some of the members that the downtime between the Fourth of July celebration and Haunted Hamlet was much too long and we needed an event that could be held each year in the early fall."

Ellie looked doubtful. "I'm not sure why anyone would come to Ashton Falls for a wine tasting. We don't even have a winery."

"Some of the event committee members suggested we do one of those wine walks, where the shops along Main Street each offer a different wine and appetizer for tasting."

"I guess that could be fun. Did the committee select someone to organize it?"

"They wanted me to do it, but I'm already doing Haunted Hamlet, so they asked a couple of the others to organize a subcommittee to do the initial legwork. My dad seems to have ended up as head of the subcommittee, so I'll probably wind up being volunteered in some capacity in spite of the fact that I still have a lot of planning to do for the Hamlet."

"Have you nailed down a venue of this year's haunted house?" Ellie inquired.

"Actually, after what's happened the past few years with the haunted house, the committee is talking about not doing a haunted house at all. Personally, I think that would be a mistake. The haunted house is the cornerstone of Haunted Hamlet. I'm not sure people from out of the area will even bother to make the trip up the mountain if we don't have one. And really, what are the odds that the event will have to be canceled due to a real dead body four years in a row?"

"Given our history, pretty good." Ellie smirked.

She had a point. Ashton Falls had seen more than its share of homicides in the past few years. Three years ago the body of a football coach from a rival high school was found in the abandoned house the committee planned to use, two years ago a real ghost hunter was found dead in that same haunted house, and then, last year, the body of one of the community volunteers was found in the very real graveyard just outside of the house we'd selected for the event. Still, in my opinion Haunted Hamlet wouldn't be Haunted Hamlet without a haunted something to serve as the cornerstone. If we didn't have to deal with unpredictable weather, a haunted hayride or a haunted walk through the woods could be fun.

The waitress came by to ask us about dessert, effectively ending our conversation.

"My stomach has been a little off lately, so I think I'll pass," Ellie informed the waitress. She turned to me. "But you go ahead."

"I guess I'll pass too," I answered even though dessert is my favorite part of any meal. The fudge cake was tempting, but I wanted to get home to check on my furry houseguests.

"I'll be back with your check," the waitress said before she left.

I was half-tempted to call the waitress back to order a piece of the fudge cake to go, but I'd been on a sugar binge lately and I knew I really should cut back. I turned my attention to Ellie. "I'm sorry you aren't feeling well. You do look a little green. I hope you aren't getting the flu."

"I'm sure I'll be fine. It's been a long month and I think I just overdid it. I haven't been sleeping all that well, which I'm sure hasn't helped the situation."

"If you remember, I had the flu at the beginning of last summer and it wasn't fun at all. Be sure to drink plenty of liquids."

"I will."

I paid the check and was gathering my things when my phone rang. I looked at the caller ID and frowned. It was the sheriff's office. Apparently, someone had ratted me out about the kittens.

Chapter 2

"Salinger," I greeted our local sheriff in our traditional manner once I'd answered my cell.

"It's Nona."

"Nona? Why are you calling me from Salinger's phone?"

"You're my one call and this is the phone they gave me to use."

"One call? Are you in jail?"

"'Fraid so and I'm madder than a cat with its tail caught in the lawn mower."

I grimaced at the imagery. "I guess Edna must have figured out that you'd taken the kittens and turned you in."

"Kittens? What kittens?"

"The kittens I found on the front doorstep this afternoon."

"I didn't leave any kittens on the doorstep, and even if I had, Edna wouldn't have turned me in. She couldn't have, on account of the fact that she's dead and all."

"Dead?"

"Deader than a doornail. Your buddy here thinks I done wacked the woman, but I didn't. I don't suppose you could come on down here and straighten this out? My shows are on in a bit and I'd hate to miss them."

"I'll be right there." I turned to look at Ellie. "They've arrested Nona for killing Edna."

"The cat woman?"

I took a deep breath as I tried to calm my racing heart. "Yeah. I have to go. Can you go to my house and check on the kittens on your way home?"

"Absolutely. Anything else? Are the kids at home?"

Ellie referred to the three minors who lived with Zak and me: Peter Irwin, more commonly known as Pi, Alex Bremmerton, and Scooter Sherwood.

"No, they're all out of town at the moment, but you should call Zak. He's out of town as well, but he has his cell. Tell him what's going on. I'll call you as soon as I know anything."

I grabbed the cute backpack I'd been using as a purse and ran for my car. Poor Nona. She was a free spirit who wouldn't do well in a cage. I hoped that once I spoke to Salinger I'd be able to get everything sorted out, although I had a feeling things were going to be quite a bit more complicated than I hoped.

The drive to the sheriff's office was accomplished in under five minutes, but it seemed like days had passed since I'd received the news. I ran in through the front door only to find the reception area empty, so I headed down the hall to Salinger's office.

"Donovan," the man with the short gray hair and steely gaze greeted me when I hurried in through his office door.

"What happened?" I took a deep breath and tried to control the panic in my voice. "Why did you arrest Nona?"

"It appears she took her campaign to shut down the kitten mill a step too far. Edna Leech is dead and we have every reason to believe Nona is the one who took her life."

I started to argue, but Salinger stopped me. "Have a seat and I'll fill you in."

I sat down on the chair across the desk from the sheriff, but I certainly didn't sit still. This really couldn't be happening. Sure, Nona was a bit of a firecracker, but she wasn't a killer. I cringed as Salinger explained that a woman named Vivian Roundtree, who was interested in purchasing one of Edna's Maine coons, had gone out to Edna's place to look at the kittens. When Edna didn't answer her door the woman decided to check out the barn; she had an appointment and she knew Edna was expecting her. When she entered the barn she found Edna dead on the floor. It was determined that she'd been hit over the head with a shovel, which they found in the shrubbery behind the barn. The police cars attracted the attention of neighbors, who were interviewed at the scene. One of the neighbors reported that she had seen a woman on a pink Harley on the property earlier in the day.

I tried to explain that Nona had been out to Edna's property that morning to check on the cats, which was when the neighbor must have seen her.

"There's more." Salinger looked at me with sympathy in his eyes. "We discovered a tassel in Edna's hand. It was determined that Edna must have pulled the tassel from her attacker's clothing when they struggled. We believe it came from Nona's leather jacket."

"How do you know that?"

"I recognized it as coming from the jacket she'd had on the day I had a conversation with her regarding the 'No Parking Zone' in town. Not too many pink leather jackets around with silver tassels."

"Oh, God." I leaned my head back and stared at the ceiling. "What did Nona say when you asked her about it?"

"She said it has been 'hotter than Hades during sinning season' and she hadn't worn that particular jacket for days. It's her opinion that anyone could have broken into the storage compartment of her Harley and taken the garment."

"Was the jacket in there when you went to look for it?"

"No. The compartment was empty. Nona seemed to think an empty compartment was proof her jacket had been stolen, but the truth of the matter is that we have no way of knowing if the jacket had ever been stored in the compartment, and even if it had been, there's no proof she didn't remove or destroy the jacket after she killed Edna."

I leaned forward in my chair and placed my folded arms on Salinger's desk. I knew I needed to choose my words wisely, but all I really wanted to do was scream at the top of my lungs that the man must be mistaken and he really should let me take Nona home. "The temperature today hovered in the mideighties. It really doesn't make sense that Nona—or anyone else, for that matter—would have been wearing a leather jacket, or any other jacket for that matter. If the tassel is indeed from a jacket, the only thing that makes sense is that someone intentionally planted it in Edna's hand."

"Maybe," Salinger admitted, "but at this point Nona is our best and really only suspect. We know she's been in a battle with the woman over the cats, which gives her motive, and she did admit that she'd stopped by the victim's home earlier this morning to confront her about some sick kittens, so that puts her at the scene of the crime."

I was sure Nona was innocent, but I saw this one was going to be tough.

"What time did Edna die?"

"It's been determined that Ms. Leech died between one and two o'clock this afternoon."

"And what time did the witness say he saw Nona on the property?"

"Before noon. I know what you're going to say: Nona might have been at the scene of the crime, but she wasn't at the scene at the *time* of the crime. The problem is that the district attorney will make the case that she came back after her initial visit and killed her. I don't suppose you can vouch for Nona's whereabouts between one and two o'clock?"

I hesitated. Nona had come home at around eleven-thirty, but she'd left again by noon, and the kittens weren't delivered to my front porch until around three. I assumed Nona had gone back for the kittens, but if she did, she clearly didn't want Salinger to know about the second visit. I supposed I understood her hesitation. Putting her at the crime scene near the time of death wouldn't help her case at all. I struggled with my conscience as I tried to determine whether or not I should mention the kittens and the fact that she must have gone back, but in the end I decided to wait. "I saw Nona this morning, but I was at the Zoo between one and two."

Salinger sat back in his large leather power chair. He seemed to be studying my face, most likely to determine whether or not I was lying. "You know how I feel about you and Zak, but I've looked at the evidence and it really does appear that Nona killed Ms. Leech in a fit of rage. The woman is a loose cannon. Do you know that she threw eggs at my car the other day after I gave her a ticket for riding her Harley down Main Street at almost seventy miles an hour? After the egg incident I brought her in to discuss the matter and she proceeded to disrobe in my office, saying if I was going to take her to jail I was going to 'have to take the real her beneath the outer layer in which we shield ourselves.'"

I suppressed a smile. "I realize Nona is a colorful person, and she has a tendency to act on her emotions without the benefit of a filter, but she isn't a killer. I know her well enough to know she has a good heart beneath the flamboyant exterior she parades around in."

"If you really believe that, you best find a way to prove it. The district attorney is convinced we have our killer, so I doubt much will be done to look for additional suspects. Personally, I think the woman is guilty. It seemed obvious to me that she was hiding something when we spoke. It would be my recommendation that you stay out of this one. For one thing, you're too close to the situation to remain objective. In the event that you don't take my advice, I would caution you to be careful. I'd hate to see you pulled into something that very well may not turn out the way you hope."

I'd rather ride Nona's pink Harley through town naked in a snowstorm than give up on her, but I didn't say as much. "I'll be careful. Can I see Nona?"

"Not until after her arraignment."

"And when will that be?"

"Tomorrow morning."

"She'll need a lawyer," I realized. "I'll arrange one."

"Figured you would. If you're unable to secure one, a public defender will be assigned, but the one in our area is newly licensed, and I have a feeling that woman is going to need someone with a bit more experience if she hopes to talk her way out of this one."

"Don't worry; I'll find someone. Is it okay to collect the cats from Edna's place and take them back to the Zoo?"

"I figured you'd want to do that, so I cleared it with the county. They want a complete inventory of the cats you remove from the property and none of them can be rehomed until we establish who legally owns them now that Ms. Leech has passed."

"Okay, I understand. And Salinger..."

"Yeah?"

"I know how it looks, but please try to keep an open mind."

"I will if you will."

I just looked at the man I had come to respect. I really hoped this wouldn't permanently destroy our relationship.

After I left the sheriff's office I called Zak, who had spoken to Ellie. He'd called an attorney he knew, who'd agreed to take Nona's case. Then I called Ellie and filled her in. She was feeling better after getting some fresh air and agreed to meet me at the cat farm to help with the relocation of the animals.

We had only about ninety minutes of daylight left despite the fact that it didn't get dark until almost nine-thirty, and I wanted to get all the animals moved that night. I finished my conversation with Ellie and called Jeremy Fisher, my assistant at Zoe's Zoo, to ask if he would be able to head there to make sure we had room for all the cats to be housed comfortably. As soon as I hung up with Jeremy, I headed to Edna's.

Edna lived on a five-acre parcel that was bordered by national forest in the back, a cabin on the right owned by a woman named Tilly Palmer, and another five-acre piece of land belonging to a man named Jethro Willits on the left. Directly in front of Edna's property, across the narrow country lane, was a seasonal ranch that offered horseback riding tours during the warmer summer months. During the winter, the owner, Ned Bunting, transported the horses down the mountain to a location at a low enough elevation that snow wasn't a factor. Maybe one of Edna's neighbors had seen someone other than Nona on the property. I'd get the cats settled in at the Zoo, then come back to knock on doors.

"Are you sure Nona is as innocent as you believe she is?" Ellie asked as she helped me load the cats into travel crates. "It makes sense that Nona came to the cat farm to rescue the kittens, Edna caught her, they struggled, and Nona ended the fight by hitting Edna over the head with the shovel."

"I know it seems like that's what most likely happened, but unless Nona confesses to Edna Leech's murder I'm not going to believe she did it. Sometimes you just have to go with your gut, and my gut is telling me that Nona is innocent. At least she's innocent of killing Edna; I have little doubt she's the one who stole the kittens."

"Even though she told you she didn't steal them?"

"Yeah, that is a bit odd. Maybe Salinger was listening in and she didn't want him to know about the kittens, or maybe she was trying to protect me from getting pulled into the whole thing."

"Are you going to add the six kittens at your house to the inventory sheet?"

Was I? Salinger had told me to keep a list of the cats and kittens I removed from the property, but technically I hadn't removed the kittens currently residing at my house. When I explained this to Ellie she shot me a look of disapproval. I knew she wouldn't say anything, but I also knew she was disappointed in me. It wasn't the fact that the kittens were valuable that made me want to hide them. I'd happily pay for them. It was the fact that at this point I really didn't know what was going to happen to the felines Edna had owned.

"What about this Aspen?" Ellie asked, diverting the subject from the kittens in my possession. "What if Nona told her about the kittens and she's the one who stole them? Maybe she's the one who actually killed Edna."

I frowned. "I don't know. She doesn't seem the type to kill a person. She's so nice."

"A lot of killers are nice," Ellie pointed out.

When I didn't answer Ellie continued with her train of thought. "Okay, let's look at the timeline. You told me Salinger said Edna was killed between one and two o'clock, which means if Nona didn't kill the woman, she had to have rescued the kittens before Edna was killed or she would have seen the body. The kittens were left for you around three. If Nona stole the kittens before Edna died she would have had to have taken them prior to two. Why would she wait to bring them to you?"

I looked out across the grassy area that fronted Edna's home. The sun had begun its descent and it wouldn't be long before the sky grew dark. I knew Ellie was waiting for me to answer, but the truth was that I didn't have one. It really did look like Nona could have done this, which was a reality I simply refused to consider. "Look, I don't know what happened exactly, but my gut is telling me that neither Nona nor Aspen are the killers, no matter that they make the two most likely suspects."

"Are you going to lie for Nona even if it turns out she did it?"

Was I? I'd like to think I'd do the right thing, but all I knew at that moment was that I was confused about where exactly the line between right and wrong was drawn. "Once I get all the cats settled in I'm going to see if I can catch the neighbors who live closest to Edna at home. Maybe someone saw something other than Nona's visit this morning."

"It's late. I'm sure the neighbors won't appreciate being disturbed. Perhaps you should plan to come back tomorrow."

"We have the events committee meeting in the morning."

"So come after. I'll come with you."

"Okay." I let out a long breath. "That sounds like a good idea."

"Are you going to be okay?" Ellie had a look of concern on her face.

"I'll be fine."

Ellie gave me a hard, Ellie hug before we began loading the last of the travel crates. I was sad that a woman had died but happy that now the cats would have the opportunity for better lives. As soon as we received the clearance to do so, we'd spay and neuter them and then find them loving homes in which to live out their lives.

Chapter 3

Tuesday, August 9

I woke up early the next morning and took the household dogs for a run before I had to get ready for the events committee meeting. The previous evening, after I'd gotten all the cats settled in at the Zoo, I'd called Zak. Originally, he wasn't supposed to be home until the following week but, given the circumstances, he'd promised to do everything he could to cut his trip short and come home as soon as he was able to arrange it. Alex was visiting her parents, who were on a dig in South America, Scooter was visiting his grandparents in Kansas, and Pi was on tour with the band he played with, so Nona and I had had the house to ourselves for a few days. Initially, I'd been looking forward to the quiet, but now I found I missed the comfort of the noise and confusion brought about by everyday routines. I was just rounding the bend where I normally turn around when my phone beeped, informing me that I had a message. I slowed to a walk and accessed my voice mail.

"Hi, Zoe, it's Nona. It looks like the fuzz have finally seen fit to release me, but I need a ride back to your place. They offered me a ride home in a police car, but I'd rather walk home naked in a snowstorm than get into one of those cages on wheels again."

I quickly hit redial and called Nona back. "Nona?"

"It's Salinger. I let your grandmother use my phone, but she refused a ride and refused to wait. She just left on foot."

"I'm out jogging, but I'm heading home. If you would be so kind as to catch up to her before she leaves the building, let her know I'm on my way and she should wait for me."

"That woman is a real thorn in my side. Asking me to go after her is asking quite a lot."

"I know, but I really want her to wait for me so she doesn't do something crazy, like try to hitchhike. I'll owe you," I said persuasively.

"Okay. But hurry. I'm not sure how much of her lip I'm going to be able to tolerate."

I ran home as fast as my short legs could carry me. I made sure the dogs had water before I grabbed my keys and headed out to my car. I might have broken a few speed limits on my way into town, but luckily, Nona was sitting on the bench outside the sheriff's office, waiting as I'd asked. I pulled into the closest parking space, then hopped out to hug the woman who, I had a feeling, was going to get us both into a lot more trouble before this whole thing was over.

"Oh my God, I was so worried," I cried as I hugged her. "Are you okay?"

"No thanks to that snake of a sheriff. Do you know, he wouldn't even let me watch my shows?"

"I set them up to tape every week after the last time you missed them," I reassured the septuagenarian. "Where's your motorcycle?"

"The fuzz took it. It's at the impound lot."

"Okay, let's get you home and cleaned up and then we'll go get it. Did the attorney Zak sent say if we needed to meet with him?"

"I don't need some expensive attorney. I'm perfectly capable of arguing my own case."

"No, you really aren't."

"But the man is just a child."

"Compared to you, everyone is just a child. Zak went to a lot of trouble to fly the guy out. We're going to trust that Zak knows what he's doing and do everything the lawyer tells us to."

"Oh, all right. We'll do it your way—for now. But not only is someone intentionally trying to set me up, the cretin stole my best jacket."

"So I heard. Are you sure it was in the storage compartment of your Harley?"

"I'm sure. It gets chilly in the evenings, so I keep it on hand."

"Do you remember the last time you wore it?"

Nona bit her lip as she considered my question. "It's been a few days at least. I remember I had it on the day it rained. I left the house early to meet up with Aspen. We planned to solicit signatures from folks in front of the market, asking for support for stricter animal cruelty laws. The sun came out shortly after we arrived, so I took off my jacket and put it in the storage space behind the seat on my bike."

"Salinger said the storage space was completely empty. Did you have anything else in there?"

Nona's eyes grew wide. "Dang nabbit. The moron who stole my jacket also took my flask. Stealing a person's jacket is one thing, but stealing a person's moonshine is something else entirely."

"Moonshine?"

"Gift from the gator wrangler I hooked up with a few nights ago."

I was tempted to ask Nona where she'd met a gator wrangler in Ashton Falls, but I had a meeting to get to so I let it go.

By the time I got Nona home and we'd both cleaned up and retrieved her Harley I was late for the committee meeting. I considered skipping it altogether so I could keep an eye on the extremely agitated woman, but she had promised to stay home and catch up on her shows and I really did want to follow up on a couple of clues she'd provided when we'd had a chance to chat. It had been my experience that the good men and women of the Ashton Falls Events Committee were more often than not in the know about what was going on in town.

The most surprising piece of news Nona had shared was that she, indeed, hadn't been the one to steal the kittens and leave them on the doorstep. My next assumption was that it had been Aspen who had taken the sickly babies, but Nona swore she'd headed over to Aspen's after she spoke to me that morning and the two of them had been together until after four o'clock, when she'd left to meet her newest conquest at the local bar. It was in the parking lot of the bar, where she'd retreated to smoke a cigar, that Salinger had picked Nona up and taken her in for questioning.

So, if Nona hadn't stolen the kittens and killed Edna, and Aspen hadn't done it either, who did that leave, other than me, on the suspect list?

When I finally made it to the meeting the wine tasting was being discussed. Ellie suggested that we sell advance tickets at a discount to encourage visitors from off the mountain to commit to the event, and make up maps so which shop would be serving which wine and appetizer would be clearly defined. It seemed that everyone in the room was focused on what can only be described as an extremely boring conversation.

I noticed Levi hadn't made it to the meeting. He'd all but stopped coming after he and Ellie broke up, although he had attended the four meetings she'd missed when she'd been away. I knew things between Ellie and Levi remained sensitive, especially now that Brady was in the picture, but the three of us had been friends for too long to let the relationship between my two best friends die altogether. In the beginning I hadn't wanted to interfere, but it had been nine months since the breakup, more than enough time, I decided, for hurt feelings to heal.

I quickly texted Levi and asked him if he wanted to come over for dinner, then texted the same question to Ellie. We were headed for a Zoe Donovan intervention.

By the time I finished meddling in my friends' lives, the discussion of the wine tasting had come to an end and Willa Walton had asked the group if anyone had anything else to talk about. I realized this was my chance to pick everyone's brain about Edna Leech's death. I started off by explaining the situation, and the fact that Nona was the prime suspect, filling the group in on the information I'd already managed to obtain. "So, as you can see, the most obvious suspects are Nona and Aspen, but they were together yesterday afternoon, so I find I'm fresh out of ideas. Does anyone have any input?"

"Are you sure Aspen and Nona aren't lying for each other?" Willa, the town clerk, asked. "They've both demonstrated a decided lack of respect for authority over the past few weeks."

"I suppose there's no way to know for certain unless a third party saw them together, but I didn't get the sense Nona was lying."

"It seems to me you should speak to this Aspen Woods before Nona has a chance to talk to her. See if their stories line up," Gilda Reynolds, owner of Bears and Beavers, a local gift shop, suggested.

"That's a good idea." I nodded. "I'll do that when we're finished here."

"You might speak to the neighbors in the area," Hazel Hampton, the town librarian and my Grandpa Luke Donovan's girlfriend, spoke up. "I know Tilly Palmer lives next door to Edna. Tilly is a very nice woman who comes into the library frequently. Based on some of the conversations she's engaged in with me and others, I think it's safe to say she's very observant, and she likes to share whatever dirt she can dig up with anyone who will listen."

"Ellie and I planned to do that after the meeting. Edna has been operating the kitten mill for quite some time. I can't imagine Tilly hadn't reported it long before Aspen found out about it."

Hazel shrugged. "It could be that she didn't think there was a problem with Edna breeding cats in her barn. Not everyone is as impassioned about our four-legged friends as you and Aspen are."

"Or maybe she did report it but, as with Aspen's complaint, it went nowhere," my father, Hank Donovan, replied. "Have you checked with the county to see if there were prior complaints?"

"Actually, I haven't. It seems, though, that if there had been, that fact would have come to light when Aspen asked them to investigate a few months ago."

"Maybe. It wouldn't hurt to ask, though."

"Yeah, I will. Did any of you actually know Edna Leech? She lived outside the town limits, but Ashton Falls is still the closest town to her property. She must have come here for groceries and other supplies."

"I remember her coming into Donovan's a few times, but we didn't really talk," Dad said, mentioning the general store he owned and operated. "I didn't realize who she was or that she was farming cats until after you became involved, and I'm pretty sure she hadn't been in since."

"Have you spoken to Scott?" Hazel asked. "If you have a barn full of cats sooner or later you're going to need the vet."

When I'd had Scott over to look at the kittens I hadn't mentioned where I'd gotten them, and he hadn't asked. I foster puppies and kittens in my home on a regular basis, so there was no reason for him to inquire.

"I haven't asked him specifically about Edna or her operation yet, but I'll stop by his place this afternoon."

After the meeting Ellie and I stopped by my house to check on the kittens and make sure Nona was behaving herself as she had promised. Other than the fact that she not only had all six kittens but one of my cats, Spade, and Alex's cat, Sasha, on the sofa with her, she was doing exactly what she'd promised to. I'd warned Nona about leaving the kittens unattended because my other cat, Marlow, was a bit of a grouch. My dog, Charlie, Ellie, and I headed over to the elementary school, where we hoped to find Aspen. School was still out for the summer, but Nona had informed me that Aspen had been spending a lot of time getting her kindergarten room ready for the new school year. I took a chance that she'd be in her classroom, and luckily, I was right.

"Zoe, how are you? Is Nona with you?" Aspen greeted me.

"No, Nona's at home watching her shows. Have you talked to her since yesterday?"

Aspen turned back toward the bulletin board she'd been working on. "No. She came by and we chatted while I cleaned up. I had a planning meeting with the rest of the staff at two, so she left, and I haven't spoken to her since. Why? Is something wrong?"

I found it suspicious that Aspen had turned so her back was to me as she spoke, but I realized she'd been at the school all afternoon the previous day, so she couldn't have stolen the kittens or killed Edna. The thing that bothered me more than Aspen's diverted gaze was the fact that Nona had told me that she'd been with Aspen until her date at four, which had clearly been a lie. I had to wonder why.

I explained about Edna's death and Nona's arrest. Aspen seemed to be shocked and dismayed and promised to help in any way she could with both Nona's defense and rehoming the cats when the time came.

"I know you've been actively protesting the kitten mill for months now. Can you think of anyone you might have met along the way who would want Edna dead?" I asked. "Maybe a fellow protestor?"

"There are a lot of people who're upset about Edna's operation," Aspen shared. "She'd been very verbal in her defense of what she was doing and her allegation that what *we* were doing should be illegal. Several of the staunchest supporters of our cause had had words with her during our protests, but I can't think of anyone who specifically comes to mind."

"Okay. Well, thanks. If you think of anything let me know."

"I will."

"I guess you can check her off your list," Ellie said when we left the campus. "It sounds like Aspen was at the school all afternoon."

"Yeah." I frowned.

"Something wrong?"

"No, nothing's wrong." I don't know why I didn't tell Ellie about the discrepancy in Nona's story. I'd trust her with my life and really had no reason to keep secrets from her, but for some reason I hesitated. "Let's head out to Edna's place to see if any of the neighbors are home. Maybe someone saw something that will give us a clue."

"Are you sure you want to get involved in this?" Ellie asked.

"Of course I do. It would kill Nona if she ended up back in jail."

"I get that, but it seems like Zak hired a really good attorney. Maybe you should just let him worry about keeping Nona out of jail."

I stopped to consider Ellie's words. The attorney did seem to know his stuff, but could I really trust him to have the skill necessary to ensure Nona's freedom when even I had doubts as to her innocence? Perhaps I needed to prove Nona was innocent for my own sake. If she simply got off due to a technicality or a superior argument made by the attorney Zak had hired and the truth was never found, there would always be a part of me that wondered.

"I know you're worried about my getting involved in yet another murder investigation, but I need to see this through. My gut is telling me there's more going on here than a simple dispute over the cats. I don't know what that might be yet, but my Zodar is encouraging me to look at the entire picture and not give in to the tendency to focus on a single motive for Edna's death—which, by the way, is exactly what Salinger is doing."

"You think someone killed her for a reason other than the dispute over the kitten mill?"

"I think the idea that Edna was killed for a different reason should be explored at the very least. Maybe we should talk to Silvia Downing. I remember Aspen telling me a while back that Silvia and Edna used to be friends. It seems in the beginning Edna just had a couple of cats who lived in the house as pets. After one of the cats became pregnant and she realized how much money was to be made selling Maine coons she began buying more and more cats until she had too many for the house and began keeping them in the barn. At that point Silvia and Edna parted ways. When Aspen began her campaign Silvia was one of her first volunteers. She not only hated the fact that the cats were treated as livestock but she hated what owning the cats had done to Edna."

"Does Silvia still work at the sporting goods store?"

"As far as I know. It's just down the street. Let's find out."

As it turned out, Silvia did still work at the sporting goods store, and she was more than happy to talk to us. Silvia, like Edna, was a very attractive woman who knew how to play up her assets and seemed to enjoy creating a reaction from the opposite sex by displaying said assets in a friendly yet seductive way. I didn't know either Silvia or Edna well, but if I had to guess, their friendship had initially been based on a mutual appreciation of outer beauty.

"Yes, Edna and I used to be friends. When we met we both enjoyed going out and partying on the weekends, but then Edna changed. Not only did she become so obsessed with her cats that she rarely left her property but she used to be kinder and less obsessed with making money. Actually, she used to be less obsessed in general."

"What do you mean by that?" I asked.

Silvia shrugged. "I don't know; it just seemed like Edna began to focus on select things and select people to an obsessive degree while pretty much ignoring everyone and everything else. It's like with the cats; she went from having a couple of them she seemed to really care about to having a barnful that, as far as I know, she cared for only to the extent they produced kittens that brought in money."

"So you decided to join Aspen in her attempt to shut down the kitten mill?"

"I was one of the first to sign up. I don't know if you've been out to Edna's place, but the way she treated those poor cats just wasn't right. And it had gotten worse. At least she used to take care of them, but lately I heard she didn't even take them to the vet when they were sick. They either got better on their own or they didn't. If you ask me, the subject of her obsession had changed in recent months. I think she was beginning to lose interest in the cats, which was why she stopped taking care of them. I'm not a psychiatrist, but I'd be willing to bet Edna had a personality disorder that could probably be labeled. After I began to hear rumors that she wasn't caring for the cats anymore I decided I would join Aspen and do what I could. The thought of sick cats left to die simply because Edna had tired of them was almost more than I could take."

Boy, did I understand that. "Do you think it's possible someone from your group could have killed Edna over the way she treated the cats?"

Silvia shrugged. "Well, I don't know for sure, but I'd be surprised if that were true. Still, there are members of our group who are very passionate about the ethical treatment of animals. Tempers do flare at times, and I know Edna had altercations with at least two of our protestors outside of their time with the group."

"Who?"

"Ben Wild and Donald Jacobs. I heard Ben ran into Edna at the post office, and Donald claims Edna has been stalking him, which in my mind totally fits."

"Stalking him?"

"I told you she can become obsessed with both things and people. I can totally imagine that if she became obsessed with a person she would stalk them. I don't know all the details, but he told me that when she showed up at the construction site where he'd been working he made it clear he was going to take action if she didn't stop following him."

I frowned. "Why would Edna be obsessed with Donald? I seem to remember he was recently engaged."

"I don't know why Edna set her sights on Donald. As far as I can tell, he didn't know either. What he said was that every time he turned around, there was Edna, watching him. It was driving him crazy. I had to stop him from becoming physically violent with her when she showed up at our protest a few days ago."

I wasn't close to Donald, but based on what I knew of him, he didn't seem like a violent man. If he'd reacted to Edna's presence in the manner Silvia had just described, the woman must really have pushed his buttons. I made a mental note to follow up with both Ben and Donald. I also wanted to have another chat with Nona.

"You know who else you might talk to?" Silvia added. "Wanda Ferguson. She isn't a member of our group, but I heard a rumor that Wanda slapped Edna at the grocery store a while back."

"Wanda slapped Edna?"

"That's what I heard. In fact, people are saying that if Ernie hadn't stepped in, their altercation would have turned into a full-on cat fight."

Okay, I guess that was interesting news. I couldn't imagine Wanda slapping anyone. She worked at the local dry cleaner, and in all the years I'd known her, she'd been nothing but pleasant. I thanked Silvia for the leads and Ellie and I said our good-byes.

If Edna had been following Donald around others must have seen her. At this point I was going to keep an open mind as I tracked down any clues there were to find.

Chapter 4

We were greeted by a young girl who looked to be around ten years old when we arrived on Edna's property. She was tall and thin, with long braids draped over her shoulders and a nose covered with freckles I couldn't help but find endearing.

"Are you here to see Edna?" the girl asked as soon as we got out of the car.

I hesitated, unsure what my response should be. "Do you live around here?"

"Just down the way." The girl pointed down the road. "I come by to play with the kittens sometimes, but when I got here today I found them all gone. Did Edna move?"

"I'm afraid Edna passed away."

"She's dead?" The girl looked to be surprised but not necessarily mournful.

"Yes, I'm afraid so."

I watched the girl as she looked toward the barn. "And the cats?"

"The cats are safe."

The girl let out a breath. "That's good. When I got here and they were gone I was afraid something bad had happened to them."

"Why would you think that?" I wondered.

"Edna told me there were bad people who were trying to take the cats away from her. She was worried about what might happen to them if the bad people got their way."

I was momentarily taken aback when I realized Nona, Aspen, and I were most likely the *bad people* the girl was referring to. "I run a shelter in town," I assured the girl. "We made sure they were all tucked in nice and comfy."

"I know who you are. You're Zoe."

"That's right. What's your name?"

"Shawna Brighton."

"So how do you know my name is Zoe?"

"My friend Tucker told me about you. He said sometimes you pay him if he finds lost animals."

"Yeah, sometimes Tucker helps me out. Do you know him from school?"

"No, I'm homeschooled, but one of Tucker's aunts lives next to me. He comes and stays with her sometimes and we hang out. Can I come to see the cats at the shelter?"

"Maybe this afternoon, if it's okay with your mother. Did you come to see the cats yesterday?"

"No. My mom made me go to Bryton Lake with her for the weekend and we didn't get back until late last night."

"When was the last time you came by to play with the cats?"

"Last week."

"Can you be more specific?"

"I guess it was Wednesday. No, not Wednesday; Thursday. I remember Tucker was here on Thursday and we came together." Shawna looked down the road. "I better go. My mom doesn't like me to talk to strangers. If she finds out that I've been talking to you, I'll get a whippin' for sure."

I looked at Ellie after Shawna had taken off down the street. "A whipping?"

Ellie shrugged.

"Let's take a walk around the property and then we can head next door to see if Tilly is home," I suggested. I stood in the drive and looked toward Edna's house. It wasn't a bad place as houses went. Two stories with green shutters, it actually had quite a bit of curb appeal in spite of the fact that it was somewhat weathered and Edna had done absolutely nothing to the natural landscape.

The barn where the cats had been housed was perhaps fifty yards south of the house. It was white as well, and from the outside it looked like any other barn in the area. If you didn't know any better, you would assume it was used for horses or other livestock; it was only after you entered the interior of the building that you realized the space was designed to house the dozens of cats Edna bred.

Ellie received a phone call shortly after we arrived so I looked around the property, then went alone to Tilly's. Unlike Edna's house, which could use a bit of TLC, Tilly's house, as well as the surrounding acreage, was immaculate. I rang the bell and waited on the front porch. The drive was devoid of automobiles, but I was sure I could hear the sound of a television coming from the back of the house.

"Can I help you?" a nicely dressed woman asked after answering the door.

"Hi, my name is Zoe Donovan."

"Oh, I know who you are. You're the shelter owner who's trying to shut down the cat factory next door."

A *cat factory* was an interesting way to refer to Edna's enterprise, but I supposed it was accurate. "Yes, I own the animal shelter in town. I was wondering if I could ask you a few questions."

"About the cats?"

"Actually, about Edna's murder."

Tilly squinted and tightened her lips. I was expecting a flat-out refusal when she opened the door and invited me in. Her home was as immaculate on the inside as it was on the outside, so I asked Charlie to wait for me on the porch.

"Can I get you a cold beverage?" Tilly offered.

"No. I'll just keep you a minute. Your home is lovely."

"Thank you. I was sorry to hear about Edna, but I wasn't sorry to find out the cats had been taken away. I was afraid they'd ruin the wedding."

"The wedding?"

"I'm getting married next month. The reception will be here in my garden, but the stench from the barn can become quite unbearable when the wind shifts and blows in this direction."

"Oh. Yes, I can see that would be a problem. Congratulations." I hadn't noticed a particular odor, but maybe that was just because I was used to the scent of animals in my environment.

"Thank you. Now what can I help you with?"

"Did you happen to notice whether Edna had any visitors yesterday?"

"I wasn't home yesterday. I left early to do some shopping in Bryton Lake and didn't return until late in the evening. I didn't even know Edna had died until Jethro filled me in this morning."

"Jethro is the man who lives on the other side of Edna's property?"

"Yes. I'm afraid Edna and Jethro didn't get along. In fact, Edna didn't really get along with any of the folks who live in this area. When Jethro showed up on my porch this morning with a big grin on his face I knew something was up."

"Jethro was upset about the cats?"

"The property line. A while back, quite out of the blue, Edna contacted Jethro and told him his well was actually on her property. Now, that well has been exactly where it is today for over fifty years, and up until now no one has given it a second thought, but Edna was thinking about adding another structure to her property and part of the permit process was to have the property assessed. It turns out the property lines on record with the county don't match the fence lines at all. As soon as Edna found out about the well, she insisted that Jethro pay her a ridiculous amount to lease the property where the well was located or she would sue."

"I take it Jethro wasn't happy about that."

"He was more than unhappy; he was downright angry. Edna wanted a fortune and his attorney told him that his only recourse if he couldn't work something out with Edna was to move the well. But the cost of filling in the old well and digging a new one a few feet away was quite prohibitive."

I had to wonder if Jethro was mad enough to kill the woman who had been causing him so much trouble.

After I left Tilly, Ellie and I headed back toward town. Neither Jethro nor Ned were at home, so I supposed I'd have to continue my investigation another day. Ellie needed to run a few errands before coming over to my place for dinner that night and I needed to go grocery shopping because the invite had been an impulse, so we parted ways but agreed to meet up at around six that evening.

The Ashton Falls Market was a small, independent store run by a friendly man named Ernie Young. Ernie liked to chat while he checked you out, so more often than not he proved to be a good source of local gossip. Actually, one of the things I liked most about shopping in the local market was the hometown feel Ernie brought to the place.

"Afternoon, Zoe. You having a party?"

I imagined Ernie's comment was prompted by the bottle of tequila and fresh limes in my basket. "No. Ellie and Levi are coming for dinner."

"I've got some nice-looking steaks on sale."

"I saw that, but I think I'm going to stick with a Mexican theme. I don't suppose you have any avocados in the back? The selection in the produce aisle are pretty hard and I wanted to make guacamole to go with the tacos."

"Hang on and I'll take a look."

I waited while Ernie went into the back. As with many small-town shops, the Ashton Falls Market was a good place to run into neighbors to discuss the latest news. Today, however, the only other customers were two women who must have been from out of town because I didn't recognize them. It only took a moment for Ernie to return with two perfectly ripe candidates. "How about these?"

"They're perfect, thanks."

Ernie and I chatted about Zak and the kids while I struggled to find a smooth segue into the topic I really wanted to discuss. Luckily, Ernie brought up Edna's death, creating the perfect opening.

"I heard she had an altercation with Wanda Ferguson right here in the store," I smoothly piggybacked onto Ernie's comment.

"You got that right. Talk about a chick fight. I thought I was going to have to call the sheriff when Edna pulled off Wanda's wig and Wanda went and slapped her."

"Do you happen to know what they were arguing about?"

Ernie looked around before lowering his voice and leaning in toward me. "Seemed Wanda was upset that Edna had been seen with her husband Pete outside the River Ranch Motor Lodge."

I frowned. "Wanda suspected Edna and Pete were having a fling?"

"Based on what I witnessed that seemed to be the case, and based on what I've heard from other folk I've discussed this with, it seems Wanda was right. I even heard talk that Pete was planning to leave Wanda for Edna. Of course, with Edna out of the way now, I'm guessing Wanda might have a shot at keeping her marriage together."

Pete was a fairly unspectacular-looking man who at first glance didn't seem the type to attract a person like Edna, but I remembered what Silvia had said about Edna's obsessions. I supposed obsessions were just that and couldn't always be explained. Wanda seemed like a nice-enough woman; still, it seemed to me a cheating husband and destroyed marriage might make as good a motive for murder as any. I wondered if Salinger knew about Wanda's feud with Edna. I considered calling him and mentioning it, but, on the other hand, knowing something he didn't could give me leverage should I need it in the future.

After the market I stopped by the feed store, which was just down the street, to get a few supplies for our household pets. Charlie began to bark and wag his entire body when we pulled into the parking lot. I'm sure he loved visiting the feed store because they always had a yummy treat for him to try out, and the people there were always nice, so he got lots of hugs and kisses as well.

"Can I help you?" I was greeted by a young man I'd never seen before. It wasn't often the feed store had new employees, but I had heard that one of the clerks had moved on.

"Hi, my name is Zoe. I run the animal rescue and rehabilitation shelter in town."

"I'm so happy to meet you," the young man gushed. "My name is Christian. Chris for short. If you just give me a few minutes, I'll gather together your regular order. I would have had it ready, but I didn't realize you'd be by today."

"You know what my regular order is?"

"Yes, ma'am. I just got promoted from handyman and delivery driver to clerk. I want to do a good job, so I made it a point to memorize the regular orders of all of our larger customers. In fact, you're our largest customer by a lot, so anything I can do for you..."

"Actually, I'm just here today to buy some food and supplies for the menagerie of animals who share our home. My assistant, Jeremy, will call first if we need to place an order for the Zoo."

The boy looked relieved. Getting together a large order like the kind we required for the Zoo would take hours for a single person.

"So, how many customers' orders did you memorize?" I asked.

"Five so far. The Zoo is our biggest client, followed by the Ashton Falls Home for Maine Coons."

"I guess they require a lot of cat litter."

"Yes, ma'am, and we sold it to her wholesale. We even delivered it, although

I heard the woman who owned the place passed away, so I'm not sure what will happen now."

I paused as two other customers came in. I realized the new clerk might know something that could at some point provide a clue, but I didn't want to start asking questions in front of people I didn't know. Charlie and I looked at the dog toys while we waited for the customers to leave, then worked my way back up to the counter.

"Looks like Charlie found a toy he likes," Chris commented.

I was more than a little bit impressed that Chris knew Charlie's name. He really had done his homework.

"Yeah, I think he's made his decision. The only other thing I really need today is dog food."

"I'll be happy to load it in your car for you."

"Thanks, I'd appreciate that. So, what did you think of Edna's breeding operation?"

"Think?"

"You said you delivered supplies there. I guess I assumed you must have had access to the cats."

"No, ma'am. Ms. Leech kept her supplies in a shed and I delivered them directly there. I asked once if I could see the cats, but she said she didn't allow anyone inside the barn except her maintenance person."

"Maintenance person?"

"The man who cleaned the pens. I met him once. Nice man."

"Do you remember his name?"

"Fritz. Don't know his last name."

"Do you happen to know his address or phone number?"

"No. It never came up. I heard Ms. Leech fired him a couple of weeks ago. I don't know for certain whether he's still even in the area. That'll be seventy-two dollars and thirty-six cents."

I handed Chris a credit card. He completed the transaction, then hauled the dog food out to my car, and I thanked him and headed home. I wished I had time to follow up on the new suspects that had come to light, but if I wanted to make it to my own dinner party on time I was going to have to investigate another day. Both Wanda Ferguson and Fritz the handyman seemed to have motives for wanting Edna dead, as did her neighbor Jethro. I was really glad these new candidates had come to light; there had been a small part of me that had begun to believe Salinger was right and Nona really was the best and only suspect.

I loved Nona. She was fun and carefree and she continually said and did things that surprised me. I hated to think she might be capable of killing anyone, but she did have a temper, and I'd seen her act without thinking on a number of occasions. The more I thought about it, the more I'd had to admit that it wasn't entirely outside the realm of possibility that Nona had gone back for the kittens and Edna had attempted to stop her, resulting in an altercation that had ended with Edna dead on the barn floor.

I decided I would put a pin in the nagging fear in the back of my mind and focus all my effort on figuring out who else other than Nona had motive to want the woman dead.

She was in the drive warming up her bike when I arrived home. "Going somewhere?"

"Gotta hot date."

I frowned. "Maybe under the circumstances you should hang out here tonight. Ellie and Levi are coming over. You can join us for dinner."

"No offense, dearie, but hanging out with a bunch of kids doesn't in any way compare to spending time with the hot cowboy I intend to lasso."

"Cowboy? I thought you were dating a gator wrangler."

"That was days ago. I figured out a long time ago that the spice of life is variety. Now if you don't mind, I need to be on my way."

I wanted to argue, but it occurred to me that Nona was fifty years my senior. Why in the heck did I think it was my job to parent her?

"Do you have your phone?"

"In my pocket."

"And money?"

"In my bra next to my emergency cigar." Nona leaned over so I could see for myself that she was telling the truth. The woman certainly knew how to work her assets.

"Okay." I gave in. "I guess you'll be fine, but please try not to be late. I worry about you."

"Oh, I'm gonna be late." Nona laughed as she climbed onto her Harley and sped away in a cloud of dust.

I rolled my eyes, but because there wasn't a thing I could do about Nona's wild ways I decided to let it go as I began unloading the groceries from the trunk of my car. I was halfway done when both

Ellie and Levi pulled into the drive at virtually the same time. I wasn't sure if the timing of their arrival was a good thing or a bad one.

"I didn't realize it wasn't going to be just us," Ellie commented as she approached my car.

"Yeah, me neither," Levi chimed in.

"Yeah, well, you know me, I'm the sneaky type." I shrugged. "I have the mixings for margaritas if you want to help me with the rest of these bags."

Both of them grabbed a bag, but I could feel the tension. I asked Levi to mix up the frozen drinks while I put the groceries away and Ellie poured chips and salsa into clay bowls. We took everything out onto the deck overlooking the lake, where I hoped, after a drink or two or ten, my friends would lighten up and remember that they *were* friends. I wasn't certain what had occurred to cause this rift. They'd seemed to be getting along just fine when Zak and I got home from Ireland in February.

I realized my search for my family tree was as good a topic as any to break the ice, so I dug in with the little information I had.

"I heard back from Clayton Longtree."

"Oh, what did he say?" Ellie asked after taking a sip of her drink.

"He's managed to trace the Donovans back seven generations, but we're a long way from knowing if my ancestor might have been the daughter Catherine gave up."

When Zak and I had gone to Ireland for a murder mystery weekend, I'd discovered that the lady of the manor back in the sixteen hundreds secretly had given up her daughter to a couple she felt would treat the child with more equality than her male-centric husband. The daughter's name was Amelia and the last name of the family she'd been given to was Donovan. At the time it had appeared that I could possibly be a direct descendent of Catherine Dunphy, and when I returned home I'd hired a man whose business was researching family trees to find out if my hunch was correct.

"Would it matter if you were related?" Ellie asked. "Would you be eligible for some sort of an inheritance?"

"No, it wouldn't matter. I'm not after any money; I'm just curious. I felt a real connection to Catherine when I was in Ireland. A part of me hopes we're related in some way."

"You felt a connection to a woman who's been dead for hundreds of years?" Levi asked.

"She felt a connection to her ghost," Ellie explained. "If you'd been around more often you would have heard the story."

"Ouch."

"Okay, guys, let's not argue," I intervened. "The three of us are friends. Best friends. I know things have been tense between you since the breakup, but you were friends a lot longer than you were a couple. I'm really hoping for all our sakes that you both can put whatever is wrong behind you."

Neither Levi nor Ellie said anything.

"Remember that time the three of us went camping and somehow managed to bring a whole bunch of stuff we didn't need but totally forgot to bring any food?"

"And Levi decided to live off the land by eating berries and tree bark, but all it did was make him sick and he ended up puking all night." Ellie laughed. "I never knew one person could throw up quite that much."

"Let's not forget the strawberry wine incident at Miller's Pond," Levi countered. "Talk about a puke fest."

"Hey, you're the one who brought the wine in the first place," Ellie reminded him playfully. "I was just a sweet young thing who had never had a drink until you corrupted me."

"Sweet young thing?" Levi countered.

"I think Zoe has us both beat with her skinny-dipping adventure after drinking that spiked punch when we were seniors in high school." Ellie laughed. "You were so shocked you fell off the side of the truck."

"I guess I had my own share of that punch." Levi chuckled.

I listened as Ellie and Levi tried to outdo each other with tales from the past. One of the best things about friendships that spanned a lifetime was that there were always plenty of stories to remind you just what an important part of your life the other people were.

Chapter 5

Wednesday, August 10

My luck, I decided, must have made a turn for the better. Ellie and Levi both lightened up quite a bit once we began sharing stories from our past, and Nona actually came home both sober and at a decent hour. I felt the stress that had weighted me down the previous day dissipate as Jeremy, Charlie, and I sat on the floor in a room filled with kittens. Jeremy and I had talked in depth about the future of the cats and kittens we'd rescued from Edna's barn, and while we had yet to be given permission to rehome the animals, we'd decided to begin the socialization process in earnest.

"I think the kittens will be fine in homes with children and other animals; it's the older cats I'm worried about," Jeremy commented as we played with the kittens and watched them play with one another. With the exception of a large male kitten who seemed fearless, most of the others were skittish when first exposed to one another, Jeremy, Charlie, and me, but the longer we played with them the more relaxed they became. "My idea is to give all the cats as much human interaction as we can manage and then decide if there are any that simply aren't candidates for rehoming. I've contacted several cat sanctuaries about taking a couple of cats each if necessary."

"I'm sure Nona and Aspen would be willing to volunteer time to play with the cats. I'll line up a few others as well. We don't currently have any large felines in residence, so maybe we can use the cougar pen as an area to socialize the cats."

"That's a good idea," Jeremy said as he tried to pry loose one of the kittens, who had decided to crawl up his back. "It's a secure pen and I'm sure the cats will enjoy having the trees to climb on. Do you have any idea what sort of a timeline we're looking at in terms of being given the all-clear to begin the rehoming process?"

"No, not really. I just hope whoever inherits them allows them to be adopted into loving, caring families. The fact of the matter is that these cats—particularly the kittens—are worth quite a bit of money. I won't be a bit surprised if the heir to this particular clowder decides to sell them rather that allow them to be put up for adoption."

"It'd be a shame if the new owner simply continued with the business Edna started."

"Yes," I agreed. "It really would."

"How are the kittens you have at your house doing?"

"Better. They seem to be responding to the treatment Scott recommended. I've been holding them as much as I can, and I know Nona has been doing the same. I think once they gain some weight they'll be good candidates for adoption."

Jeremy laughed as two kittens chased each other across the room and ended up in his lap. "I love my job. I mean really, what other job pays you to play with kittens?"

Jeremy set the kittens aside and began carefully walking around the room to ensure that all of them were participating. "Have you managed to come up any new leads into Edna's murder?" he asked as he picked up one of the kittens that had been shying in the corner.

"Maybe. I haven't had a chance to speak to the new suspects on my list, but it seems Edna was having an affair with Pete Ferguson."

"Pete? Really? He doesn't seem the type."

"I totally agree, but according to Ernie, who's usually in the know, not only was Pete having a fling with Edna but he had plans to leave Wanda for her."

Jeremy whistled. "Sounds like motive for murder to me."

I set the kitten I was holding down and picked up another. 'That's what I thought. The only other suspects I've managed to dig up are Edna's neighbor, who had been fighting with her over the property line, and a man named Fritz. It seems he was Edna's handyman until she fired him."

"I know Fritz. He came in looking for a job after Edna canned him. We didn't need anyone, but I gave him a couple of leads."

"How did he seem?"

"Seem?" Jeremy asked.

"Did he seem like a killer?"

Jeremy shrugged. "I'm not sure how a person who's a killer would seem, but he wasn't carrying a weapon or anything. He did seem pretty upset about getting canned. Apparently, part of his pay was supposed to come from a percentage of the money made off the sale of the kittens, and he was pretty sure he wasn't going to see any money from the litters last housed at the facility."

"Seems odd to pay a handyman with a percentage of sales," I pointed out.

"I think he was more than a handyman. It sounded to me as if he was more of an assistant, or even a manager."

A man who was not only fired but who felt he was being gypped out of a profit that was rightfully his would make a strong suspect, I decided. Maybe I'd take some time that afternoon to pay a call on the bitter ex-employee. If Fritz had applied for a job with us, we should have his contact information on file.

"By the way, how did your trip with Jessica go last weekend?" I asked.

Jessica was Jeremy's girlfriend, the mother of a seven-year-old girl named Rosalie who absolutely adored Jeremy's two-year-old daughter, Morgan. My mom and dad had watched both children the previous weekend so Jeremy and Jessica could have a special trip away.

"It went great. In fact," Jeremy's face broke into a grin, "Jessica and I are engaged."

"Oh my God." I got up from the floor and crossed the room. "I'm so happy for you." I hugged Jeremy. "Why didn't you tell me before now?"

"Jessica wanted to wait for us to announce it until she had a chance to tell her family, but I figured I can trust you to keep our secret."

"Absolutely. Have you set a date?"

"Not yet, but I'll let you know as soon as we do. In fact, I was kind of hoping you and Zak would let us hold it at your house. You have such a nice setting for a wedding."

"You can absolutely hold it at the house." I hugged Jeremy again. "I'm so excited for you. I think you, Jess, Morgan, and Rosalie are going to make an awesome family."

Jeremy really did look happy, which made me happy too. He'd had a tough time as a single dad, but things had gotten so much better for him once Jessica came into his life.

"I hear someone in the front." Jeremy turned his head and looked toward the door. "I think Tiffany is up there, but she did say something about cleaning the bear cages, so I'd better check just in case."

Tiffany Middleton was one of our most trusted employees at Zoe's Zoo.

Jeremy left the room and I turned my attention to Charlie, who had not one but four kittens crawling on his back. He was such a patient dog. No matter how many times he was hissed at or swatted in the face, he continued to lay on the floor with what can only be described as a smile on his face.

I took my phone out of my pocket and pulled up a new note. There, I listed the suspects I wanted to try to speak to that day and the reason I believed they had motive to kill Edna. Fritz had been fired from his job and gypped out of the pay he probably felt he had coming to him, Wanda believed her husband had been stepping out on her with Edna, and Jethro had reason to want Edna out of the way to avoid digging a new well that was over his property line. I looked at the list and considered whether there were others who ought to be added. I remembered Aspen saying Donald Jacobs was convinced Edna was stalking him, so I added his name. Aspen had also told me Ben Wild had had words with Edna when they'd run into each other at the post office.

So far that gave me five new suspects, which was five more than I'd had when I started. Not bad, I decided, for a day and a half of sleuthing.

"Delivery for Zoe Donovan-Zimmerman." Jeremy returned from the front with the largest bouquet of flowers I'd ever seen.

"Uh-oh," I replied as I glared at the colorful display.

Jeremy frowned. "Someone sends you a fantastic bouquet and all you can say is 'uh-oh'?"

"It's not my birthday or my anniversary and I haven't been ill, so a display of this size delivered on a random weekday morning can only mean one thing."

"'I love you'?" Jeremy tried. "Or maybe 'I miss you'? Zak has been out of town for over a week."

"A single rose means *I love you*, a small display means *I miss you*, but a bouquet of this size can only mean *I'm sorry*."

Jeremy looked more closely at the flowers. "I don't see a card. Maybe you have a secret admirer."

I crossed the room after setting the kitten I was holding on the floor. Jeremy was right; there was no card, but I knew the flowers had to be from Zak. "Something tells me I'd better call Zak."

"Go ahead and use my office. I'll start putting the kittens away," Jeremy offered.

Unfortunately, Zak didn't pick up when I called. I knew he was busy trying to get things wrapped up so he could come home from his trip early. If there was something really bad going on he'd call me. Wouldn't he? Maybe the flowers were simply an *I'm sorry* for not being here to deal with the Nona situation.

"I just got off the phone with Scott," Jeremy informed me when I returned to my office. "He wants you to bring the kittens you have at your house by his office this afternoon if you have a chance. A couple of the blood samples he took seem suspicious and he wants to take another look."

"Suspicious? Suspicious how?"

"He didn't say. I'm sure he'll fill you in when you stop by."

I glanced at Charlie, who had wandered over to sit next to me. He'd been so patient, but I could tell he was ready to call it a day. "I'll head home and get them now. Call Scott back and tell him I'm on my way."

I sure hoped nothing serious was wrong with those babies. It'd only been a couple of days, but I was already attached to the little fur balls. There was one orange-and-white kitten in particular who had wormed his way into my heart. Marlow would have a fit if I brought yet another cat into the family, but I had to admit that given enough time it was going to be close to impossible to let the little guy go.

When I arrived at home I noticed a strange car in the drive. I began to get an even worse feeling about the bouquet that had been delivered as I considered the possibilities. The car could belong to someone visiting Nona, but the feeling of dread that I couldn't quite quell convinced me that our visitor was someone worthy of a bouquet costing several hundred dollars.

My worst fears were confirmed when I walked into the house. "Mrs. Zimmerman?" It took every ounce of control I had to keep from hyperventilating as the artfully dressed woman paused to look me up and down.

"Really, dear, now that you're Zachary's wife you really should pay more attention to your personal grooming. You look like a street urchin."

"I was at the Zoo playing with kittens, a job that really doesn't require designer clothing. What are you doing here?"

"I heard Nona has been causing you problems and I'm here to help."

Oh no, no, no. This wasn't good. This wasn't good at all. Zak's mom didn't like Nona, and as far as I could tell, the feeling was mutual.

"That's very sweet of you," I managed to croak out, "but I think I have everything under control. There really isn't any need for you to stay. I know how busy you are."

"Nonsense. Nona is a Zimmerman, and if there is a problem with a Zimmerman you can bet a Zimmerman will take care of it."

"Nona isn't a Zimmerman," I pointed out.

"Yes, well, close enough. Now which rooms can we use?"

"Rooms? As in more than one?"

"Nona can be a handful, so I brought help." Mrs. Zimmerman smiled, as if she were delivering the best news in the world instead of the worst.

"Help?" I felt my heart drop clear down to my feet.

"Darlene is home from college and Twyla and the kids weren't busy, so they offered to come along. Isn't that nice?"

"They're *all* here?" I know my voice sounded high and squeaky. Zak's cousins Twyla and Darlene were sisters. Darlene was single, but Twyla had two very undisciplined children who'd almost destroyed the house the last time they'd visited.

"They are and they have all given up three weeks of their summer to help out, so be sure to give them nice rooms. Preferably overlooking the lake."

"Three weeks!" At this point I'm pretty sure I blacked out. Well, maybe not physically but definitely mentally. The cousins had all stayed at the house the previous summer when they'd come for Zak and my wedding, and if I remembered correctly, they'd all spent their time lounging around while Zak and I waited on them. If the cousins had returned you could bet it had more to do with a free vacation than a rescue operation.

I wanted to say something that would make this all go away, but I knew there wasn't anything I could say, so I closed my eyes and counted to twenty.

"You look a little pale, dear," Mother Zimmerman commented. "Are you feeling all right?"

Not by a long shot. "I'm fine. Are the others here already?"

"Yes, we came together. They are all in the pool."

"And Nona?"

"She left shortly after we arrived. She said something about an appointment."

Smart woman. Leaving sounded like an excellent idea. "I also have an appointment," I announced as firmly as I could manage.

"You should poke your head in to say hello before you leave again. It is the polite thing to do."

"I would, but I'm really late. I'll say hi to everyone when I get back."

With that, I ran up the stairs with Charlie on my heels. I transferred the kittens into a travel crate and then Charlie and I headed back to the car. Knowing Mother Zimmerman would find a reason to detain me if I dallied in the least, I headed toward the main highway and then pulled over when I felt it was safe and tried to call Zak again.

"Please pick up, please pick up, please pick up," I chanted as I waited for him to answer his cell.

He didn't pick up.

I left a rather abrupt and slightly less than loving message before hanging up and deciding what to do. The only thing I could do was to continue on to the veterinary hospital and hope the reason Zak hadn't picked up was because he was flying home. I was about to restart the car when my phone rang and Zak's number flashed across the screen.

"Donovan here."

"Ouch. I guess you got the flowers."

"I did, just before I came home to find out your mother and cousins had settled into our house for the remainder of the summer."

"Didn't you get my message?"

"What message?"

"I tried to warn you. I called and left a message on both the house phone and your cell after I received my mother's message this morning."

I glanced at my cell. There *was* a message I hadn't yet checked, and I hadn't been home to retrieve the message from the house phone. "I didn't get the message. I was busy playing with the kittens."

"Kittens?"

"I'll explain later. Please tell me you're on your way home because if I have to deal with your relatives on my own in addition to keeping an eye on Nona, blood is going to be shed."

"I'm trying to get home as soon as I possibly can, but I've run into some problems and I really can't get there any sooner than Friday. When I found out what my mother planned I tried to call her back to tell her to check into a hotel, but she didn't pick up."

"Of course she didn't. Did she know you're out of town?"

"She did."

"So the timing of her visit was intentional."

"It looks like it. I'm so sorry."

"She said she was here to help with Nona. How did she even know what happened with Nona?"

"I may have mentioned it when I spoke to her yesterday," Zak said sheepishly. "You know I love you more than anything. I'll figure out a way to get her out of the house and into a rental as soon as I get home."

I sighed but didn't respond.

"If I could get home sooner I would."

"Yeah, I know. We'll be fine."

"I was supposed to meet with my client twenty minutes ago, so I really have to run. I'll call you this evening."

"Okay."

"I love you."

"I love you too."

I remembered a friend telling me, before I married Zak, that when you got married you weren't only marrying the man you loved but his family as well. Boy, was she right. I took a deep breath to calm my nerves and then pulled back onto the highway. My stress over Mother Zimmerman and the cousins was quickly replaced by fear about the kittens in the backseat and the reason Scott wanted me to bring them in.

Scott was an awesome man I considered to be not only my veterinarian but a friend. He was currently dating Tiffany Middleton. Scott had donated much of his time to us, especially when we were first starting out and didn't have a big budget.

"So?" I asked anxiously after walking into Scott's office with my cat carrier.

"Several of the kittens have an elevated level of white blood cells. There could be many reasons for that, but the most common is infection. Given the overall health of the kittens, I want to start them all on an antibiotic. I'll have you bring them back in a couple days and we can do another blood test to see if they're responding to the drug. How are they eating?"

"Pretty well." I picked up the smallest kitten. "This little guy needs quite a bit of coaxing, but I think we're making progress."

"The formula I gave you to supplement their food is high in both nutrients and calories. They should all be gaining weight. I'm going to weigh them all again today. We'll need to keep an eye on their progress. If the antibiotics don't take care of the white blood cell issue we'll need to look for other causes."

Scott weighed each kitten as well as doing a complete exam for them. Then he gave me the medication I would need and encouraged me to get as much formula into the babies as they would tolerate. We arranged to meet up again on Friday and I left the animal hospital, debating what to do next. Twyla's children reminded me of a Tasmanian devil: They were loud, undisciplined, and overly energetic. I figured the family cats knew plenty of hiding places to stay out of harm's way, and Zak's dog, Bella, and Scooter's dog, Digger, were both large enough to be capable of fending for themselves, but I had an overwhelming need to protect Charlie and the kittens. I could keep Charlie with me, but I couldn't crate the kittens all over town while I went about my daily chores. I could leave them at the Zoo, but Jeremy had his hands full, and the kittens really did need extra attention. After some thought I decided to see if Ellie would keep them for a few days. The boathouse she lived in with her dog Shep was small, but the kittens really didn't take up much space and Ellie was the most nurturing person I knew.

Ellie's home had originally been converted by my grandfather for me. When I'd moved in with Zak I rented the boathouse to Ellie rather than sell it. I loved the small space that was my first home away from home. It's weathered and unconventional, with a large living area, a small loft bedroom, and a modern yet cozy kitchen. The entire wall facing the lake had been replaced with glass to give the space an open, airy feel.

I called ahead to make sure Ellie was there and willing to foster the kittens for the time being, so she was waiting for me on the deck, which looks out over the lake. As I pulled up in front of the boathouse I suddenly had a flashback to a year earlier, when the Zimmerman clan had descended on the house and I'd likewise run to Ellie for shelter. So much had happened since then. I felt I had grown as a person, and my love for Zak was stronger than ever. I vowed in that instant not to let Mother Zimmerman drive a wedge between us now as she had back then.

"Sorry to hear you've been invaded." Ellie hugged me as Charlie, the kittens, and I joined her on the deck.

"Yeah, me too. Can you believe they plan to stay three weeks? What am I going to do?"

"Zak managed to get them moved once he returned home last summer. I'm sure he can do the same now as well. Chances are Mrs. Zimmerman knows Zak will ask her to move into a rental, which will make him feel guilty, thereby giving her leverage over him for whatever she's really after."

"You think so?"

"That'd be my guess. The woman is crafty."

Yeah, I realized, she really was. "I still need to go back to the house to pick up the medicine and supplements Scott gave me in the beginning, but I didn't want to risk Twyla's spawn seeing the kittens and insisting on playing with them, so I brought them by here first."

"That was probably a good idea. The kittens are welcome to bunk with Shep and me for as long as they need to. You and Charlie are as well."

"Thanks; I just might take you up on that. Zak won't be home until Friday. That's two whole days for me to go completely over the edge and strangle his mother."

Ellie laughed. "I trust you to control yourself, but really, if it gets bad come over."

I chatted with Ellie for a few more minutes before I headed home to get the supplies she'd need for the kittens. Everyone was outside either in the pool or on the beach, so I was able to sneak in and out without anyone noticing. I did notice Nona's bike was still gone, which had me mildly concerned. After I got the kittens settled in with Ellie, Charlie and I would have to try to track her down.

Chapter 6

Finding Nona proved to be a futile task. She wasn't answering her cell, Aspen hadn't seen her, and I didn't find her downing shots at her favorite bar. The only thing to do was to leave a message on her voice mail and then focus my energy on interviewing the new suspects I'd identified. I only had a few hours to snoop around because Mother Zimmerman had requested my presence at dinner, and while I'd rather walk across hot coals than attend, I knew it would be rude to ignore the woman completely.

I figured Wanda would be the easiest to track down because I was pretty sure she'd be at work on a weekday afternoon. Of course I had no idea how I was going to broach the subject of her husband's infidelity with the woman who'd been murdered, so I ran into the local dress shop, bought the least expensive item I could find that required dry cleaning, and then drizzled the soda I had in my car down the front of it. Then I headed to the dry cleaner and prayed Wanda would be in and I hadn't just ruined a perfectly good dress for nothing. Luckily, Wanda was both at the counter and alone when I arrived.

"Hey, Zoe; Charlie. It's not often we see you in here."

"Yeah, well, jeans and T-shirts don't really need dry cleaning. I do have this dress, however. I spilled something on it and just as I was about to toss it in the washer I noticed the dry-clean-only tag."

Wanda looked at the label. "It's a good thing you didn't wash it. It would have been ruined for sure. What did you spill on it?"

"Grape soda. Do you think you can get the stain out?"

Wanda frowned as she studied the stain, which had dried quickly thanks to the afternoon's heat. "It'll take some work, but I can get it out. Next week okay?"

"Yeah, that's fine."

Wanda began to write up a ticket.

"I don't suppose you've seen Zak's grandmother this afternoon," I said as I waited for my receipt.

"You mean the one who rides the pink Harley?"

"Yeah, that's her."

Wanda shook her head. "Been here all day, and I have a clear view of the street. I didn't notice her pass by. She missing?"

"Not really, but she got some upsetting news and I want to make sure she's okay. I guess you heard she was arrested for Edna Leech's murder."

Wanda didn't say anything, but her eyes got big. It seemed obvious this fact was news to her.

"Salinger let her go because he didn't have enough to hold her, but I'm pretty sure she's the main suspect unless they track someone else down," I added. "I don't suppose you have any idea who might have wanted Edna dead?"

Wanda furrowed her brow, stopped what she was doing, and looked at me with an expression of suspicion on her face. "Why would you think I would know? I barely knew the woman."

"Oh, I'm sorry. I saw Edna and Pete together a while back and I guess I just assumed Edna was a friend of the family."

I watched Wanda's face as it turned bright red. She visibly fought for control before she spoke. "Pete was simply discussing a business deal with Edna. We aren't personal friends, although if you ask me, the world is better off without the likes of Edna Leech in it. Still, I'm sorry to hear about Zak's grandmother. If she's innocent I'm sure things will get straightened out when they find the real killer."

"That's what I'm counting on." I lowered my voice, as if I was about to share a secret. "I heard the killer left some DNA on the shovel used to kill Edna. I'm sure it's only a matter of time until Nona is cleared."

Wanda frowned. "DNA?"

I picked a piece of candy out of the dish on the counter and tried to appear disinterested and casual as I unwrapped it and popped it into my mouth. "I don't have all the details, but it seems there was blood from two different people on the shovel: Edna's and someone else's. Salinger is assuming Edna fought back and the killer was injured."

I studied Wanda's face as she processed this piece of information. She appeared to be interested but not panicked. Maybe she wasn't the killer I was looking for. Of course if it got back to Salinger that I was making up fake evidence he'd be the one killing me. "Of course," I added, "it may be that the whole story of the DNA is simply a rumor. You know how people like to make things up."

Wanda handed me my ticket and promised to call me when the dress was ready. It was obvious she no longer wanted to talk about the murder, and if her husband had been sleeping with Edna, she seemed to want to cover that up as well, but I wasn't picking up the guilty vibe.

I left the store and headed over to Pete's insurance office to see if his reaction to my fake news was different from that of his wife. Maybe Pete was the bad guy. It could be that he was sleeping with Edna but had decided to break if off and she hadn't taken it well. A love affair gone wrong had certainly been the motive for murder many times before.

Pete Ferguson hadn't always been an insurance salesman. When he and Wanda first moved to Ashton Falls he'd worked for the power company as a meter reader. Several years ago he was bitten by a dog while on duty, and he'd insisted he was unable to do his job as a result of the trauma he'd suffered. He'd sued the power company and was awarded a small settlement, which he used to open his own insurance office. Zak and I personally don't buy our insurance from Pete, but he seemed to get by, so I could only assume there were others in the community who were willing to look past the fact that he tended to deal in fly-by-night insurers in order to take advantage of the cutthroat prices he was able to come up with.

"Afternoon, Pete," I greeted as Charlie and I walked into his office.

"Surprised to see you here. Last time I talked to your old man he accused me of writing phony policies."

"Yeah, well, I'm not here about insurance." I decided the direct approach might be my best option in this instance; Pete still held a grudge against Zak and I could see small talk wasn't an option. "I'm here to talk about a murder."

"Should've known you'd be snooping around in Edna's death. Never in my life have I met anyone who's as much of a busybody as you."

"Yup, that's me, Zoe the meddler."

"Well, whatever it is you think you know, you're wrong. Now, if you'll excuse me, I have work to do."

"Look, I know all about your affair with Edna and the way you tried to break it off and she went all *Single White Female* on you." Taking a huge leap and making this particular allegation was a risk, but sometimes you just had to toss bait in the water and wait to see who bit. "What happened? Did you try to talk some sense into Edna? I bet she went berserk, it got physical, and in your own defense you picked up the shovel and hit her."

"No matter what you think you might know, I didn't hit Edna. In fact, I wasn't anywhere near her place at the time she was killed."

"But you were involved with her?"

Pete sighed. "Hooking up with Edna was a huge mistake. It cost me my marriage and a good chunk of my savings. It isn't something I want to discuss with you or anyone else."

"Your savings?"

"Did you miss the part about my not wanting to discuss this?"

"You can talk to me or I can tell Salinger what I know and you can talk to him."

Pete took a deep breath that he let out very slowly. Then he motioned for me to have a seat. "I guess if you're intent on meddling you should have the whole story, but I'm going to ask that you refrain from repeating this. It really is both embarrassing and demoralizing."

"As long as what you tell me doesn't lead me to believe you're guilty of Edna's murder, I agree not to repeat it." I sat down on the chair on the visitor side of Pete's desk.

"It all started back in June," Pete began. "I met Edna when she came in about some insurance to cover her livestock."

"Livestock? You mean the cats?"

"Yes, the cats. Do you have any idea how much they're worth?"

"Quite a lot. Go on."

"We seemed to hit it off. At that point there was nothing inappropriate going on, but it seemed over the next few weeks that we kept running into each other. Every time we met Edna would flirt a little and I would flirt right back. A few days before the big Fourth of July celebration she called and asked me to meet her at the River Ranch Motor Lodge outside of town. She said her car had broken down and she needed a ride. When I arrived she greeted me in a skimpy nightie."

"So you slept with her."

Pete ran his fingers nervously through his hair. "Yes, I slept with her. I hadn't gone to the motel with that intention, but Edna was an attractive woman and my marriage had been on the rocks for quite some time. I knew right off it was the wrong thing to do. In spite of the problems we've been having I love my wife. I tried to break it off with Edna, but instead of understanding and walking away she informed me that she had photos of our time together and she would show them to Wanda unless I gave her five thousand dollars."

"What did you do?"

"I panicked and paid her off."

"And did that end things?"

"For a while. And then a few weeks ago she called me and said she needed another five thousand dollars. She wanted me to bring it to the motor lodge. When I arrived there I told her I didn't have that kind of money, and if she showed the photos to Wanda or tried to get more out of me I'd prove she'd blackmailed me. She seemed surprised that I'd turn the tables on her, and in the end we agreed to call it even and move on with our lives. The problem was that one of Wanda's friends saw Edna and me leave the room at the motor lodge at the same time and she went directly back to Ashton Falls and told her."

"And then?"

"And then Wanda hit me with a frying pan."

I had to fight the urge to laugh.

"After she threw half the dishes in the cupboard at me we talked about what had happened and agreed to take a break while we figured out whether our marriage could be saved. I made it clear I wanted us to work on our relationship and put the whole thing behind us, but I could tell Wanda didn't believe I was really through with Edna. During that time-out Wanda ran into Edna in the grocery store, and I guess you heard what happened there."

"Yes, their fight has been the topic of conversation on the Ashton Falls gossip network ever since Edna died."

"I know it seems as if Wanda has a tendency toward violence. First she hits me with a frying pan and then she attacked Edna. But I promise you she wouldn't have hit Edna with a shovel, if that's what you're thinking."

Actually, I hadn't been thinking that, but now that he mentioned it, it did seem Wanda had a habit of striking out at people who angered her.

"I feel like such an idiot. Wanda wouldn't be dealing with any of this if I hadn't let Edna seduce me."

"Well, maybe now that Edna's gone you have a chance at saving your marriage."

"I sure hope so. The woman means the world to me. I'm lost without her."

I looked directly at Pete. "If you didn't kill Edna and Wanda didn't kill Edna, do you know who might have?"

"You might want to talk to Donald Jacobs."

Donald's was one of the names Aspen had given me. I remembered her saying Edna had been stalking him, but I wanted to see what Pete might say. "Why would Donald kill Edna?"

"Because the crazy bitch was stalking him the way, I now realize, she'd been stalking me. I was gullible and I really believed she just happened to need groceries at the same time I did, and that it was just a coincidence that we ended up in the same line at the DMV. I've been married a long time and having a single woman flirting with me fed my ego. I was such a fool. After I gave her the five grand and broke things off she began stalking Donald and I could see the whole thing was a con. She wasn't into me at all. It seemed to be her pattern to find men to sleep with and then blackmail them. I was going to warn Donald, but I didn't need to. He wasn't as gullible as me. He made it clear to her from the beginning that he wanted nothing to do with her."

"Yet it sounded like she continued to stalk him."

"Yeah. As odd as it seems, the more he resisted her charms, the more determined she seemed to be to conquer him. If you ask me that woman was about to send him over the deep end."

"So you think he finally flipped out and killed her?"

Pete appeared to be considering my question. "Edna could get under your skin. She had a way of making a person do things he might not otherwise have done. If you talk to Donald keep in mind that if he did kill Edna, in my mind he was totally justified."

As Charlie and I walked back to my car, I had to wonder how the murder of a kitten mill owner had turned into something so much more. If it wasn't for the fact that the kittens had been left on my doorstep shortly after Edna was killed, I'd go out on a limb and theorize that the kitten mill didn't play into her death at all.

I was tempted to try to track down Donald right then, but a quick glance at the clock on my dashboard informed me that I'd best leave that interview until the following day if I didn't want to be late for my dinner with Mother Zimmerman and the Zimmerman cousins. Of course by the time I endured a dinner out with the Zimmermans it might be me in jail for murder. I know it seems as if I absolutely hate my mother-in-law. It isn't really that I hate her. She'd brought Zak into the world and for that I would always be grateful. It was more that the woman seemed to know exactly which buttons to push to make me want to run from the room screaming every time I talked to her. When Zak and I had married I'd vowed to find a way to get along with his mother, but there were times, like now, when I truly doubted my ability to keep that vow.

It was late by the time we got home from dinner. I had just crawled into bed after making sure all the household animals were safely tucked away in my bedroom when my cell phone rang. My initial thought was to hope it was Nona, who I still hadn't heard from, but I was just as happy when I saw my late-night caller was Zak.

"Hey," I said tiredly as I snuggled down under the covers. "It's late. Even later where you are. I didn't think you'd call."

"I'm sorry." Zak yawned. "I wanted to call earlier, but I was in the middle of coding the program and didn't want to stop. I'm really trying to get finished in time to get home by Friday."

"I appreciate that. I'm all snuggled up with the three dogs and three cats, but I miss not having you to snuggle up with at the end of the day."

"Yeah." Zak sighed. "Me too. Every time I have to travel lately I find myself vowing to either sell the company or turn things over to a full-time manager."

"You'd probably get bored after a while," I said.

"Maybe not. Once the main campus of Zimmerman Academy opens I'm going to have plenty of things right there in Ashton Falls to keep me busy."

"That's true. I guess we can talk about it some more after you get home and your mother is relocated so that we have the house to ourselves."

Zak yawned again. I could tell he was fighting to stay awake. He was probably lying in bed like I was. How sad that we weren't together.

"How did things go today?"

"Okay. Salinger let Nona out of jail, but I'm pretty sure she's still the main suspect. I've been working on a few theories of my own that could take her out of the limelight altogether if they pan out."

"You aren't doing anything dangerous, are you?"

"No," I assured my worrywart husband. "Not dangerous. I'm just talking to people in public places in the middle of the day."

"Maybe you should just let Salinger handle this one. Even when you don't mean to put yourself in danger you seem to end up in the middle of it, and it worries me that I'm not home to rescue you."

"Don't worry. I'm not doing anything that might lead to anyone needing to rescue me." I decided it was best to change the subject. I really didn't want him to worry about my getting into trouble, so I decided to give him something else to worry about. "I had dinner with your mother and cousins tonight."

"You did? I figured you would be hiding out at the boathouse with Ellie."

"Trust me, I thought of doing just that, but I didn't want to be completely rude. I did manage to avoid them for the bulk of the day, though."

"So how did it go?"

"Actually," I turned slightly to make room for Spade on the pillow next to me, "it wasn't too bad. At first. Darlene went out of her way to act as a buffer between your mother and me, and Twyla managed to control her kids so they didn't disturb the other diners."

"And then?" I could hear the sound of dread in Zak's voice. "You said *at first*."

"And then your mother informed me that she'd hired a contractor to remodel the guest bedroom next to ours. It seems she thinks it's time we turned the room into a nursery."

"A nursery? We aren't even pregnant."

I could tell by the irritation in Zak's voice that I had successfully distracted him from my participation in Edna's murder investigation. "I know that and you know that, but according to your mother we're behind schedule."

"There's a schedule?"

"Apparently. According to your mother, now that our one-year anniversary has come and gone, it's time to begin working on popping out Baby Zimmerman number one. According to her, if we don't start immediately we'll be much too old to raise a child once we get to baby number four."

"*Four*?"

"Yup. She has it all planned out. She even has a chart that shows the number of months it takes for the average couple to conceive once they begin trying, the gestation period of the average fetus, and the ideal length of time between each pregnancy."

Zak actually laughed.

When I'd decided to distract him with the story of the ridiculous conversation I'd had with his mother I'd thought I was past my own irritation. Apparently, I was wrong. "Why are you laughing? Not only am I furious that your mother has arranged for a nursery to be built in our house without even asking either one of us first but when she started asking whether my cycle was regular and if I'd discussed the ideal sexual position for conception with my doctor right in the middle of the restaurant I thought I would die."

"I'm so sorry," Zak said in a somewhat more serious tone. "Really. If I could be there this minute I would. It's Wednesday night; I'll be home Friday. Please just try to avoid my mother as much as possible until I get there."

"Trust me, after tonight's dinner I plan to." I was tempted to hang up, but the last thing I wanted to do was hang up mad, and I had after all been the one to bring up the subject of the nursery in the first place. "Did you talk to Alex today?"

Alex, who was in South America with her archeologist parents, was due to return to Ashton Falls within the next couple of weeks, and Zak had informed me during a previous conversation that he'd arranged to speak to her about her plans the next time she was in cell phone range.

"Yes."

"How did she seem?"

"She said she'd had a nice visit, but she missed us and was ready to come home. I spoke to her mother, who agreed the visit had run its course, so I sent Coop to get her." Coop was the private pilot Zak used. "After he picks her up he's going to come get me, so we both should be home on Friday."

"Really?" I grinned. I'd missed all the kids, but especially Alex. Suddenly my irritation with Zak's mother and my fear over Nona's part in Edna's murder was replaced with pure, unadulterated joy. "That's wonderful news."

"I thought that might bring a smile to your face. I really need to get a few hours' sleep so I can finish this project tomorrow. I'll call you in the morning if I get the chance."

"Okay. I can't wait to see you. I miss you."

"Yeah," Zak said in a tired-sounding voice. "Me too."

Chapter 7

Thursday, August 11

When I woke up on Thursday morning I decided to take the dogs out for a run. A glance at my bedside clock confirmed it was early yet, so I quickly dressed in a warm pair of sweats and shepherded the dogs outside before anyone else awoke and waylaid me.

I headed down the beach toward the boathouse. Even in the summer mornings tended to be cool in Ashton Falls, but it was actually quite pleasant in the sun today. Maybe if Ellie was awake I could talk her into breakfast on the deck overlooking the lake. When I lived in the boathouse Charlie and I enjoyed many breakfasts looking out over the crystal-clear blue water. We had a great deck off the back of the house Zak and I now owned, but the little deck behind the boathouse faced the east, providing the earliest sun along this particular stretch of beach.

Luckily for Charlie and me, Ellie was both awake and dressed when we arrived. She was sitting in the sun with a blanket wrapped around her, staring blankly into space.

"It looks like I'm not the only early bird on the beach this morning," I greeted her as my dogs greeted Shep.

"Couldn't sleep, so I decided to come out for some fresh air. Can I get you some coffee?"

"I'll get it," I offered. "There's no reason for you to get up. Do you need a refill?"

"No. I'm fine."

When I went in through the side door of the boathouse I noticed Ellie had created a play area for the kittens where they had room to wander and yet were contained so as not to toddle off into trouble. I knew she was the perfect person to take care of them while the cousins invaded my house. Ellie was the sweetest and most nurturing person I knew.

I poured my coffee and returned to the deck, where Ellie was still staring into space. It was early and she might just be tired, but I had a feeling it was something more.

"Something wrong?" I asked.

"I've just been feeling funky lately. I thought I had the flu, but my symptoms come and go, yet it doesn't seem to be going away."

"Maybe you should go to the doctor."

Ellie yawned. "Yeah, maybe. I looked my symptoms up on the Internet, and according to what I found, there are all kinds of horrible diseases that fit the profile."

"I think those medical sites are dangerous in the hands of nonmedical professional. Call your doctor. Maybe you're just anemic."

"Yeah, maybe," Ellie repeated. "How's the murder investigation going?"

I sat back in my chair and tucked my feet up under my legs. The early morning sun was shining brightly, creating tiny sparkles of light on the perfectly glassy water. "I'm not sure. I'm coming up with a lot of leads I didn't expect. Edna was an interesting person. And I don't mean that in a good way. It seems she had a toxic personality that rubbed pretty much everyone the wrong way. Do you know she actually stalked Pete Ferguson until he slept with her and then blackmailed him with photos she'd taken of the two of them in bed?"

"I don't know how much stalking Edna had to do to get Pete into bed. She was an attractive woman and Pete has a wandering eye. Still, the blackmail thing is somewhat surprising and a classic motive for murder. I wonder if she'd done that before with other men."

"I don't know if Edna had stalked and blackmailed men prior to Pete, but when I spoke to him he said she turned her sights to Donald Jacobs."

"You think Edna was blackmailing Donald?"

"As far as I know she wasn't. Pete said Donald wasn't falling for her seduction. Still, you make a good point about other men prior to Pete."

"I guess you could mention it to Salinger. It might be worth looking in to."

"Maybe I will, although to be honest, at this point I'm pretty much avoiding him. I'm afraid he's going to ask me questions about Nona I don't want to answer, and I really hate to lie to him."

"And you shouldn't. Lie to him, I mean. He's helped you out a lot in the past and you have no reason not to trust him."

Ellie made another good point, but until I figured out exactly how Nona fit in to all this I really didn't want to have a conversation with Salinger. Given Ellie's contemplative mood this morning, it occurred to me it might be best to change the subject. I wondered if she'd heard about Jeremy. Probably not or she would have brought it up. It was really too bad I'd promised Jeremy I wouldn't talk about the engagement. It would make a perfect topic of conversation to lighten the mood.

"Did I tell you Mother Zimmerman is having a nursery built in our house?"

Ellie looked surprised. "Is there something you haven't told me?"

"I'm not pregnant. Zak and I haven't even begun to discuss that situation with any real seriousness, but Zak's mom has decided that now that we're past the honeymoon phase of our relationship it's time to get on to the baby-making one."

Ellie laughed. "She really told you that?"

"She really did. She even took the time to design graphs and charts with gestation periods and time averages to achieve conception. When she asked me about the regularity of my monthly cycle in the middle of the restaurant I thought I was going to die."

"Oh, that's funny." Ellie chuckled. "What did Zak say?"

"He said he'd handle it when he got home."

"And he will, I'm sure. Thanks for the laugh. I needed one."

"Any time my embarrassment can brighten your day I'm happy to share it."

"I'm sure it wasn't that bad."

"Oh, no, it was. You know how that woman's voice carries. She had everyone in the restaurant staring at us. She even went so far as to suggest Zak and I become more deliberate in our lovemaking."

"Deliberate?"

"More mindful of the timing and positions we choose."

"She brought that up in the restaurant?"

"Twice."

Ellie got up and gave me a hug. "You were quite the brave woman to have married Zak even after meeting his mother. Though I guess it could be worse. Mrs. Zimmerman is a busybody who can be downright rude at times, but she isn't really mean and she does love her son."

"Yeah, I guess. I'll still be glad when her visit comes to an end."

"I don't blame you one bit." Ellie gathered up the blanket she'd been using. "I guess I should go inside and feed the babies you've left in my care."

"I'll help you. I'm not in a hurry. I noticed the play area you set up for them."

I got up and followed Ellie inside after calling all the dogs onto the deck.

"I figured it would make sense for them to have a place to play where they were contained so I didn't have to worry about them. I'm really enjoying the little buggers. That one little orange one is so sweet. And such a cuddler."

"Yeah, he's a sweetie. Maybe if we get the approval to adopt them out you can keep him."

Ellie got a faraway look on her face. "Maybe. Shep seems to get along okay with the kittens, and I do love to listen to a good purr. This is going to sound crazy, but there are times when I wake up in the middle of the night and miss the sound of Levi snoring."

I picked up the first kitten and began the process of dropping the medicine Scott had given me into his mouth. "It was fun with the three of us hanging out the other night. It's been a long time since it's just been you, me, and Levi."

"I guess. I did have fun, but it still feels odd to hang out with him as just friends."

"You seemed to be getting along okay when you worked together on that murder case while Zak and I were in Ireland. Did something happen?"

"No," Ellie denied. "Nothing happened. I'm starting to feel funky again. Could you finish this? I'm thinking about going back to bed."

"That's a good idea and I'm more than happy to finish, but when you wake up you be sure to call the doctor."

"Yes, Mother."

Ellie went upstairs, I finished feeding the kittens and giving them their meds, and then the dogs and I headed home. I really wasn't in the mood to deal with Mother Zimmerman and the cousins, and happily, they were all still asleep. I fed all the animals, showered, and changed into a comfortable shirt and shorts and was just heading down the stairs with Charlie when Nona came in from the kitchen.

"Where have you been?" I scolded her.

"Avoiding the wicked witch and her trained monkeys."

I tried not to smile; that was so mean but so funny. "I was worried about you. Why didn't you at least call to tell me what you were doing?"

Nona frowned. "You were worried?"

"Of course I was worried. Didn't you even listen to the million phone messages I left?"

Nona smiled. And not in the evil, I've-got-something-up-my-sleeve way I was used to but an actual smile. "I guess I'm not used to having anyone to worry about me. I've been alone a long time."

"Well, you aren't alone anymore. At least not as long as you're here with us, so if you're going to take off for hours on end please let me know where you're going."

Nona did something she had never done before. She reached out and hugged me. She almost broke a rib, but I could tell it was genuine.

"So where are you off to?" she asked.

"I was going to follow up on a few leads I picked up yesterday in Edna's murder case."

"Then I guess that's where I'm off to as well. I'll drive."

"I was going to bring Charlie."

"Okay, you can drive, but I've got shotgun."

"I'm sure Charlie will be fine with that."

I still wanted to speak to Donald Jacobs; Ben Wild, who had been seen arguing with Edna at the post office; Fritz, who'd been fired by her, and Jethro Willits, the next-door neighbor. I figured a mere argument wasn't much of a motive, so I decided to interview Ben only if the other leads didn't pan out.

I knew Donald was working on the new office building in town, so he seemed the easiest of the three remaining suspects to track down. When I arrived at the construction site I made Nona agree to wait with Charlie in the car. I parked in the shade and rolled down all the windows before promising not to be too long.

There was a fairly large crew working on the office building so it took me a few minutes to locate Donald. I was afraid he wouldn't be able to take a break to speak to me, but when I offered him a paper cup filled with frosty iced tea, he indicated that he was well overdue for a fifteen-minute cool down.

"I'm going to go out on a limb and guess you didn't just stop by to bring me a cold drink," Donald said after drinking half the tea in one long gulp.

"No, I didn't stop by just to bring you a drink. The truth is, the tea is just a bribe I hope will persuade you to talk to me about Edna Leech."

Donald made a face that indicated the sweet tea had suddenly taken on a sour taste. "What do you want to know?"

"I heard that prior to her death Edna had been following you."

"Stalking is more like it. The woman was seriously disturbed. I made it quite clear from the very beginning that I wasn't interested in what she was peddling, but she refused to take no for an answer."

"Did you think about getting a restraining order against her?" I wondered.

"Thought about it a time or two, but Edna was real careful about where she'd show up. The fact that she popped up so often seemed to me to be a clear indication that she was following me, but she was careful only to show up in public places where she could claim she had reason to be. Besides, I hate to say it, but I was embarrassed to tell the sheriff that I needed him to protect me from a teeny, tiny woman like Edna."

"Yeah, I guess I can see that. Do you know who might have killed her?"

"No. Should I?"

"There are those who are suggesting maybe you got tired of her harassing you and decided to handle things in a permanent sort of way."

Donald shook his head. "When I heard what happened to Edna I knew there would be folks who would think I did it. I certainly did threaten her in public on a number of occasions. But I didn't follow through on my threats to kill her. And if I had, I wouldn't have taken a shovel to her head and then left the murder weapon lying around for someone to find. If I'd killed Edna it would have been a methodically planned assault that wouldn't have left any evidence. A shovel is a weapon of opportunity that suggests the attack wasn't planned to me," Donald continued. "A premeditated murder would more likely have involved a standard weapon like a gun or a knife, or poison. Seems to me you're looking for someone who would have cause to be on her property for a reason other than a planned murder, who got mad and hit her with the shovel in a spontaneous act of passion."

Donald made a good point. The way Edna had died, and the fact that the murder weapon was abandoned close by, didn't speak of someone who had come to the property with the intention of killing a woman so many people loved to hate. Why use a shovel as a murder weapon for any other reason than proximity?

I chatted with Donald for a few more minutes and then returned to the car where Nona and Charlie were waiting.

"What now?" Nona asked after I started the car and turned on the air conditioning. It wasn't a particularly hot day, but I didn't want the interior of the vehicle to have a chance to heat up.

"I need to talk to one of Edna's neighbors. I guess we'll head out there next. If Jethro is home, you and Charlie can get out and walk around while I chat with him."

"Are you sure you don't want me to help with the interrogation? I've been known to scare the pants off a few men; I suppose the same tactics will work to scare the truth out of them."

"Thanks." I smiled at the imagery the feisty woman always seemed to conjure up. "But I think I can handle Jethro if you'll keep an eye on Charlie."

I probably should have called ahead before driving all the way out into the county but I wasn't sure Jethro would want to talk to me, and if he didn't, I didn't want to give him the opportunity to refuse to see me. My plan at this point was to show up at his door and start asking questions.

While Tilly's home was spotless and Edna's was somewhat worn but basically kept up, Jethro's property was a mess. Old cars and other items he must have collected over the years littered most of the open space between his house and the road. I parked in front of Edna's place so

Nona and Charlie could wander around without getting lost in Jethro's junkyard, then carefully made my way through the junk to the front door of the run-down house.

I rang the bell and waited. I didn't hear any noise coming from inside the house, but there did seem to be someone wandering around at the back of the lot. When no one answered the door I chose the clearest path I could find between the old vehicles and headed toward the sound I'd heard.

"Jethro," I said to the man, who had his head under the hood of one of the cars.

"Who's asking?" he asked after looking up.

"Zoe Donovan. We've met a couple of times."

"Yeah." The man wiped his grease-stained hand across his face, creating a black streak across his cheek. "What do you want?"

"I wanted to talk to you about Edna."

"Hmph," the man growled. "As far as I'm concerned, the woman got what she deserved. Dang-nabbed property line."

"I heard you had a disagreement over your well."

"My well is two feet on her side of the line. The woman had five acres and she was having a fit over two feet she wasn't even using and didn't care a lick about until she found out she owned it. I hate to speak ill of the dead, but all I can say is good riddance."

"I understand moving the well would have been a huge undertaking."

"Now that there is an understatement. There's no way I have the kind of money it would take to redig the dang-gummed thing."

"I heard Edna offered to lease you the property."

Jethro wiped off the wrench in his hand with a rag he had draped over the fender of the car he'd been working on. "What is it you said you wanted?"

I didn't feel as if I could simply ask the guy if he'd killed Edna, but I really didn't have a way to ease into such a delicate question. "I was wondering if you were home the day Edna died."

"Yeah, I was here. What of it?"

"Did you happen to see anyone on her property that day?"

"Yup, several folks. Guessin', though, that what you're really asking is whether I saw Edna's killer."

"Yes." I nodded. "I guess that is what I'm asking."

"Then the answer is no. I have no idea who killed the woman and if I did, I wouldn't tell you or anyone else. Now, if you don't mind, I have work to do." Jethro stuck his head back under the hood of the car.

When I told Nona he wasn't talking she rolled her eyes and instructed *me* to wait for *her.* I tried to convince her we should simply be on her way, but she shook her head and took off toward Jethro's house like a woman on a mission. When she returned ten minutes later with the answers I'd been unable to obtain, I realized she might make a better sleuthing partner than I'd been giving her credit for.

"So?" I asked when we were back in the car and heading back toward town.

"Seems after I left and before the woman who came to buy the cats and found Edna dead arrived, Jethro went into town for a burger and saw Fritz Moon's truck parked down the road."

"Fritz had as much reason as anyone to want Edna dead," I said.

"Jethro indicated that Fritz was an okay guy, but he did have a temper, and he was understandably mad that Edna was trying to gyp him out of money she rightfully owed him. He also pointed out that if Fritz was here on legitimate business he would have just parked in the drive rather than down the street. Jethro shared that there's a footpath that leads from the spot where he saw the car parked to the back side of Edna's barn."

"Why is it that Jethro told you all this but wouldn't talk to me?" I complained.

"I'm guessing you don't know how to ask a man what it is you want to know."

I rolled my eyes as Nona leaned forward, showing off just a bit of her cleavage. She certainly wasn't one to act her age, which I supposed was one of the things I loved the most about her.

I called Salinger and filled him in on what we'd learned. He said he'd follow up with Jethro when he had a chance, and also mentioned that the coroner had found some irregularities, so he was taking a second look at both the timeline and the cause of death. He promised to let me know if there were any significant developments and, again, asked me politely to be careful and not take any unnecessary risks.

"I met a man at the bar last night who used to know Edna before she turned into the crazy cat woman," Nona shared as I drove her back to the house.

"Oh, and did he have anything interesting to say about our victim?"

"Not really; only that she used to be a real party animal until she became obsessed with the cats and stopped showing up at the bar."

"Edna's ex-friend Silvia said something similar. I wonder if something happened to Edna that would account for the personality change."

"You mean like how I used to be an old stick in the mud and then one day I woke up and was suddenly awesome?"

"Yeah, something like that." I remembered Zak telling me that Nona used to be a curmudgeon who made everyone's life miserable and then, one night about ten years ago, she went to bed an unhappy old woman and woke up the next morning a free-spirited hippie. The doctors attributed the change in personality to a stroke of some sort.

A stroke, or some other similar physical event, might explain how a woman could suddenly develop the tendency to fixate on objects such as cats and certain men to the point of compulsion. I supposed the why behind Edna's strange behavior was something we might never know.

I dropped Nona off at the house and was about to head over to Ellie's to check on my sick friend when I received a call from Jeremy, letting me know that we had a nuisance dog call from the new bakery on Main Street. He wondered if I would be able to respond because his sitter had dropped off Morgan at the Zoo while she went to a doctor's appointment. I told him I'd be happy to respond and headed in that direction.

When I arrived at the bakery I was informed that the dog was guarding the Dumpster out back and would growl whenever anyone approached. The bakery owner told me he'd tried to shoo it off with a broom with no success. I had my car rather than my rescue truck, so I hoped I'd be able to deal with the animal without the use of my gear.

"Hey," I greeted the dog softly. I immediately noticed that she'd recently delivered puppies, which led me to wonder if the pups were hidden nearby. The dog was skinny and mangy, so I assumed she'd been on the street for quite some time.

I put Charlie on his leash and slowly removed him from my car. The mama dog growled. I took some dog treats from the stash I kept in my glove box and gave one to Charlie while I spoke to him softly. I could see the mama dog watching me. I told Charlie to stay while I slowly made my way toward the Dumpster with a fistful of treats.

"I'm not going to hurt you, sweetie. I just want to help you, and if you have pups nearby I want to help them as well."

When I got to within five feet of the dog she began to growl. I stopped walking and tossed her a treat. She looked at it suspiciously before sniffing and finally eating it. I took one step closer. She positioned herself between me and the Dumpster. I tossed her another treat. With each treat I threw, I took another step closer. Eventually, I was within reaching distance. It seemed odd to me that the dog was still guarding the Dumpster when I had readily available food and had made it clear I was willing to share.

"I'm going to look inside to see what it is you're so intent on guarding," I softly informed the dog. She growled deeply in the back of her throat, but I didn't get the sense I was in any real danger as long as I trod carefully, so I took the final step and looked inside.

"Oh my God," I whispered when I saw four puppies that couldn't be more than a day or two old laying amid the trash. I slowly reached in and picked up the first pup. It still felt warm, and I could feel its little stomach move as it took a breath. I turned and slowly showed the mom that I had one of her babies. "We need to get your babies to the vet. I'm going to help you, but you need to trust me."

The mama seemed to understand what I'd said, and she let me lead her over to my car. I opened the back door and set the puppy on the seat. She looked toward the Dumpster and then back toward the puppy. "I'll get the others, I promise." The dog hopped inside the car and began licking the puppy, which began to whimper. It only took me a minute to retrieve the other three pups, which were likewise alive. I did a quick search to make sure there weren't any other pups, then put Charlie on the front seat and headed toward Scott's.

Chapter 8

"Who would toss puppies in a Dumpster?" Ellie asked later that evening, when I'd stopped by to see how she was feeling.

"I don't know, but if I catch whoever did it I'm going to be the one wanted for murder."

"Are the puppies going to be okay?"

"Scott says yes. He's keeping both mom and pups at the veterinary hospital for a few days so he can keep an eye on things. He didn't think the pups had been in the Dumpster all that long; probably only a couple of hours. If the bakery owner hadn't called to complain that the dog wouldn't let him get near the Dumpster they would have died for sure."

Ellie picked up one of the kittens she was fostering and held it to her chest. "Sometimes I wonder what's wrong with people. I'm going to assume someone found the pups shortly after they were born and tossed them in the Dumpster, which is really the only explanation as to how they got there. What I don't understand is how the mom let them get to the pups in the first place."

"Maybe the mom left the pups to look for food or water and they were already moved when she got back. Or maybe, even more disturbingly, the pups were put in the Dumpster by someone the mom trusted. It's impossible to know for sure, but I plan to ask around to find out if anyone saw anything."

"What's going to happen to them after Scott releases them?"

"I'll take the mom and pups home until the pups are old enough to be adopted and then I'll find homes for all of them. After what the mama dog has been through I'm going to make sure I find her an awesome home with someone who will love her and care for her."

"Is she a small dog or a big one?"

"Small. About Charlie's size. Why? Are you in the market for another dog?"

"No, but maybe you should talk to Willa. She doesn't really seem like she'd be the type to want to have a pet, but we were talking a while back and she mentioned she'd been thinking about getting either a cat or a small dog."

"I'll talk to her. She can be a bit stricter than I'd prefer at times, but I know she has a kind heart and she's definitely responsible. I'm sure our mama would be happy living with Willa after being out on the street."

"Poor thing. When I hear about things like that it just breaks my heart." Ellie wiped a tear from her cheek. "When I think what could have happened…"

"Is anything else wrong?" I asked. Not that finding puppies in a Dumpster wasn't something to cry over, but it looked like the pups were going to be fine, so tears at this point weren't really called for.

"Not really. I've just been feeling emotional lately. I called the doctor today and I have an appointment to see him tomorrow."

"That's good. Maybe your hormones are off or something. I was thinking of calling in an order for a pizza. Extra sausage?"

Ellie made a face that indicated that pizza didn't sound all that appetizing.

"I suppose if your stomach is all funky I can make you something. Scrambled eggs? Pancakes?"

"Why don't you go ahead and pick up whatever you want for dinner and I'll figure something out for myself?" Ellie suggested.

"Are you sure? I can get you anything you want."

"I'm sure."

"I'm not all that hungry. Why don't we relax out on the deck for a bit and figure out the whole dinner thing later?"

Ellie didn't say anything, but she accepted the glass of water I offered her and then followed me out onto the deck.

"How did your sleuthing go this morning?" Ellie asked.

"It looks like Fritz Moon might be the killer I've been looking for."

Ellie frowned. "Fritz? Really?"

"Do you know him?" I asked. Until Chris from the feed store had mentioned his name I'd never heard of him.

"I don't know him well, but he used to come into the Beach Hut for lunch sometimes. He knew Tucker somehow, and the two of them would eat burgers and talk about television shows they'd both seen or the newest action flick out in the theater."

"Didn't you find it odd that a grown man would be friends with an eleven-year-old boy?"

"Not really. Tucker might be eleven, but he's a very street-smart eleven. As you know, he doesn't have a lot of parental supervision, so he's in town on his own fairly often. I think Fritz is just a nice man who somehow met Tucker and decided to take him under his wing. If it turns out he's your killer, I'm going to be very surprised."

I remembered that Tucker sometimes came to see the cats with Shawna, the girl I had met at Edna's that first morning after the murder. I guess it made sense that if Fritz once worked for Edna, Tucker would have met him during one of his visits. So far I hadn't had any luck tracking down Fritz, but maybe Tucker knew where I could find him. It certainly wouldn't hurt to call him to ask. Normally, Tucker spent a lot of time at our house, but I hadn't seen him once since Scooter had left to visit his grandparents. I knew his mother worked two jobs, so chances were I'd find Scooter's best friend at the video arcade. Maybe after I got some food down my best friend I'd stop by to see if he was there.

"Do you know how long Fritz worked for Edna?"

Ellie squinted as she thought about it. "I'm not really sure, but it seems he started coming around the Beach Hut with Tucker about a year ago. Other than to take his order, I really never spoke to him. The only reason I know what they talked about is because Tucker tends to be loud, so I could overhear parts of their conversation."

"It might be worth my time to track Tucker down to see what he knows. I haven't seen him since Scooter left town, but he usually hangs out at the arcade."

"When is Scooter coming back from his trip?" Ellie asked.

"I'm not sure. He'll be home in time to start school, but I'm not sure how long before that he'll be home. Alex is coming home tomorrow with Zak, though." I smiled.

A wistful look came over Ellie's face. "I'd love to have a little girl to do things with the way you do with Alex."

"Did you ever in a million years think I would be the one excited about shopping for school clothes?"

Ellie smiled. "It is odd the way things worked out. I've wanted to be a mom since I was a young child and you used to say you were never having kids, and yet, for all intents and purposes, you have three children while I don't have any."

I reached out and squeezed Ellie's hand in a gesture of support. "You're more than welcome to go school clothes shopping with me and Alex. I know she'd love to have you."

"Thanks. I might take you up on that."

"If you had a bigger place I'd suggest you take in some of the academy students the way Phyllis, Ethan, and a few of the others have, but you really don't have the room."

"No, I don't, and I love living in the boathouse, so I'll just borrow Alex when I feel the need to feed my maternal instincts. Do you know how her visit went? I know she wasn't all that thrilled about going in the first place."

"Zak didn't say. I guess we can ask her about it when she gets back." I looked toward the drive when I heard the sound of a car pulling up. "Oh, look. It's Levi and he brought pizza."

Ellie turned green.

"You don't have to eat it, but I'm starving."

"I thought you said you weren't hungry."

"I lied." I stood up and greeted Levi. "You must have read my mind."

"I heard the Zimmerman clan was in town and I figured you'd be hiding out here," Levi said. "I took a chance on the fact that you hadn't eaten yet."

"I haven't and I'm starved." I took the pizza from Levi's hand. "Grab some plates from inside. I'll get some drinks."

By the time we got everything set out Ellie's shade of green had faded and she looked mostly normal. She still didn't feel like eating pizza, so Levi made her one of his special grilled cheese sandwiches. Ellie always had craved his grilled cheese when she was sick, and I could tell it meant a lot to her that he remembered.

We talked about general subjects such as the new construction project in town, the upcoming wine tasting, and this year's football team. I updated Levi on the opening of Zimmerman Academy and he told us all about the new staff they'd hired at the high school. All in all, it was a fun and relaxing evening. Levi insisted that Ellie go to bed early, which she promptly agreed to do, and I decided to head over to the arcade to see if I could track down Tucker. Levi offered to come along and I readily accepted.

"Ellie seemed distracted this evening," he observed as we drove toward the arcade. We'd decided to drop my car at my house and ride into town together.

"I don't think she was feeling all that well. It seems like this flu bug has been hanging on for a while. I'm sure she'll be fine soon."

"Maybe. I've known Ellie a long time, though, and I'm pretty good at distinguishing sick Ellie from worried Ellie."

"She got on the Internet and started looking up all the horrible diseases she might have. She has a doctor's appointment tomorrow. I'm sure he'll find out she just has the flu and that she worried for nothing."

"Maybe."

Oh, great. Now Levi looked worried.

"Zak is coming home tomorrow," I said, changing the subject to something safer. "He mentioned that he wanted to get together with you to discuss the best way to integrate sports into the Academy's curriculum."

"I'm available," Levi informed me. "Maybe we can grab dinner or something."

"I'd like that," I responded as he pulled up in front of the arcade. "I hate to leave Charlie in the car alone. Why don't you wait here with him? I'll go inside and if Tucker's there I'll see if he wants to go for ice cream or something."

"Okay. But hurry. I'm not sure this parking spot is entirely legal."

Luckily, Tucker was inside and was more than happy to come with Levi and me for ice cream.

"When's Scooter coming home?" Tucker asked as he dove into the triple scoop sundae he'd insisted he must have.

"I'm not sure. Within the next couple of weeks for sure," I replied.

"It's boring without him, especially now that Fritz is gone."

"Ellie mentioned to me that Fritz sometimes buys you lunch. Have you been friends long?"

Scooter shrugged. "A while. He used to work down at the kitten place, and me and Shawna used to go visit, but he doesn't work there no more. Can I get something to drink?"

"How about some water?" I suggested.

"A Coke?"

"I think that sundae will cover your sugar requirement for the day."

"Okay, water's fine."

Levi motioned to the waitress to bring it.

"A friend of mine told me he saw Fritz at the kitten mill on Monday. I wanted to talk to him about that. Do you know how to contact him?"

"Nope."

"You said he was gone. Do you know where he went?"

"Nope."

"Did he tell you when he'd be back?"

Tucker looked up from his dessert. "Is Fritz in trouble?"

I didn't answer.

"Does that mean he is in trouble?"

"Maybe," I admitted. "I can't be sure until I talk to him."

"Fritz said he might be in trouble on account of the dead lady, but he didn't do it."

"He told you he didn't kill Edna Leech?" I clarified.

"He didn't have to. I was with him when we found the lady."

I frowned. Was Tucker with Fritz on Monday? "Maybe you'd better tell me exactly what happened."

"Am I going to be in trouble too?"

"Did you do anything wrong?" I asked.

Tucker put his spoon down and looked directly at me with a tear in his eye. "I don't want to go to jail."

I put my hand over his. "Why don't you tell me exactly what happened? You can trust me." I looked at Levi. "You can trust Levi too."

"Yeah, buddy," Levi added. "What's going on? Did something happen when you were with Fritz?"

Tucker looked at Levi and then back at me. "We didn't mean to do nothing wrong; we just wanted to help the kittens."

"The kittens?" I asked.

"The ones me and Fritz brought to your house."

"You stole the kittens?"

Poor Tucker looked terrified. "Am I going to jail?"

"No, you aren't going to jail. Why don't you start at the beginning and tell me everything that happened? Don't leave anything out."

Tucker told us that when he and his friend Shawna went to visit the kittens the previous week they'd noticed that some of them were sick. They'd asked Edna about them, and she'd said the mother had died and the kittens would probably have to be put down. Tucker wanted to save the kittens, so he went to Fritz and asked him to help him steal the kittens and bring them to me. He knew I would help them. Fritz agreed to go with him, so they drove out to the county and parked on the road. Then they snuck around the back through the forest.

When they went into the barn they found Edna dead on the floor. Tucker swore Fritz was as surprised as anyone, and that he had no idea what had happened to the lady. I asked him why they didn't call the sheriff and Tucker said Fritz was concerned that he'd be a prime suspect, given his quarrel with Edna over the money she owed him. As far as Tucker knew, Fritz had left the area and had no immediate plans to return.

I took Tucker home and called Salinger to fill him in on what I'd found out. You'd think the man would be happy I was basically doing his job for him, but instead he chewed me out for being in possession of the stolen kittens all along and just now getting around to mentioning it. At least he agreed to let me keep them while they straightened everything out. I just hoped whoever ended up having the say-so as to what would happen to the kittens would let me keep them until I could find them good homes.

I thought about the pups I'd rescued that day. Sometimes being a rescue worker was difficult and depressing work. There were times we didn't arrive on time and had to deal with our sorrow for the needless deaths of our four-legged friends. But today had been a good one. Today good had prevailed over evil, and I meant to cherish the victory and worry about the times things didn't work out as well when I was confronted with them.

Chapter 9

Friday, August 12

In spite of everything that was going on and the myriad of emotional issues I was dealing with, I woke with a smile on my face. Zak and Alex were coming home today. It seemed the family had been scattered over the summer. I was looking forward to school starting up and a return to our regular routine.

Pi wouldn't be with us this year. Zak had arranged for him to graduate high school early and he'd been admitted to one of the top colleges in the country. I'd miss his daily presence in our lives, but I knew moving on with his education was the best thing for him.

Scooter would be in the sixth grade at Ashton Falls Elementary and Alex would attend Zimmerman Academy on a full-time basis. We'd hoped to have the main campus up and running by the start of the school year, but a winter with heavy snow had delayed the construction of the project, so the temporary building we'd used the previous year would have to do again. Zak was frustrated by the delay, but in the long run I thought having an additional year to hire staff and admit students would actually be beneficial.

I crawled out of bed and dressed in a pair of sweatpants and a sweatshirt. Although the high for the day was supposed to hover around eighty, the morning temperature was a cool thirty-eight degrees. I knew once the sun came up over the mountain it would actually be pleasant, so I made a cup of coffee and took it out on the deck, where I could keep an eye on the dogs as they romped on the beach.

When I'd gotten back home the previous evening Twyla and Darlene had been in the media room watching a movie and, based on her absence from the living area of the house, I'd assumed Mother Zimmerman already had gone to bed. Nona hadn't been home by the time I turned in, but her motorcycle was in the drive this morning, so I assumed she'd been out partying and had gotten in late.

"You're up early," Mother Zimmerman said, walking up from behind me.

I turned and looked at my mother-in-law, who was dressed in fuzzy slippers and a warm bathrobe. "I have a busy day, so I figured I should get an early start."

"It seems you've been gone almost the entire time we've been here."

I took a sip of my coffee before answering. The last thing I wanted to do was to start my day with an argument. "I wasn't aware you were coming, so I didn't have the opportunity to schedule my time differently."

"Yes, I suppose you have a point. I spoke to Zak last evening and he reminded me that we had agreed I would give adequate notice prior to visiting. It is his opinion that I owe you an apology for showing up unannounced, so consider this my apology."

"Thank you."

"Zak also informed me that I had overstepped my boundaries by arranging to convert your guest room into a nursery without speaking to you first. I canceled the contractor I'd hired."

"I appreciate that."

"You do plan to have children?"

I looked at Mother Zimmerman. "Yes, Zak and I plan to have children. When we're ready."

"I know it must seem as if you have all the time in the world to take on the responsibility of parenting, but time flies by faster than you can imagine. Don't let the fact that you are fostering the children who live with you prevent you from the joy of having children of your own."

I tucked my legs up under my body and turned to look at the woman who, like it or not, was going to be the grandmother of any children Zak and I had. "Before Alex and Scooter came to live with us I was certain I didn't want to have any children of my own. Ever. But having these two awesome kids in my life has caused me to look at things differently. It's because of them that I'm now open to the idea of having children. Instead of looking at the kids as an obstacle to the grandchildren you hope to have one day, maybe you should get to know them. You may find you actually like them."

"Yes, well, perhaps you are right. It's a bit chilly. I think I'll head indoors."

I turned back toward the lake as soon as Mother Zimmerman left. I really hadn't given all that much thought to when Zak and I might take the next step and bring a baby into the family. Maybe I'd talk to Zak about it when he got home. I knew he really wanted a child, although to be honest, I wasn't sure this was the right time. We were both so busy with our businesses, the Academy, and the two children with whom we already shared our home.

Then again, maybe Mother Zimmerman was right. Maybe time did fly by and waiting for the perfect time might mean we'd miss our window. This was a complicated matter that would require a lot of thought, definitely not something I'd find an answer to today.

When I was satisfied the dogs had worn themselves out I headed inside to shower and dress for work. I planned to spend a good part of the day at the Zoo, making sure the cats we'd taken guardianship over were settling in as comfortably as could be expected. I also had two cubs who were scheduled for release in the fall that I needed to assess, and I needed to relocate a raccoon family that had taken up residence in the crawl space under the building.

If I had time I also wanted to follow up with the only "suspect" still left on my list: Ben Wild. An argument at the post office didn't necessarily denote a motive, but maybe he would have some sort of insight that would point me in a new direction.

"I have great news," Jeremy said to Charlie and me an hour later.

"I love it when the day starts off with great news. What's up?"

"There was a message on the machine from the attorney handling Edna Leech's estate. He said the heirs aren't interested in the cats, so we're free to rehome them. He's sending over a signed release this afternoon."

"That is great news." I tossed my backpack on my desk chair. "Have you identified any of the cats that might be ready for new homes right away?"

Jeremy handed me a list. "All the cats on the list show adequate socialization skills to be integrated into homes, although I think we'll need to find applicants who're looking for indoor-only cats. These have never been outdoors and I doubt they'd have the instincts needed to survive the predators in this area."

Personally, I recommended that all the people who adopted our cats raised them indoors, but there were a number of cat owners in the environs who chose to ignore that recommendation. Some cats had the instincts to survive the coyotes and cougars living around Ashton Falls while others didn't.

"Once we get the written release let's go ahead and put an ad in all the usual places, letting people know that we're taking applications for the cats," I instructed Jeremy. "We need to make it clear that all of them will be altered prior to adoption. That should weed out backyard breeders hoping to make a buck. After you do that, call Scott to schedule the spays and neuters. Oh, and have him do a medical evaluation for each cat as well. We want to be sure the animals we adopt out are healthy." I picked up a pile of mail and started to weed through it. "Anything else I should know about?"

"I got a call from Fish and Game asking if we could take a couple of bear cubs that were orphaned when their mother was shot by poachers. The bear cage is at capacity until we release the two older cubs this fall, but if we can move the cats out of the cougar cage we could temporarily house these cubs in there."

"Do we have anywhere to house the cats?"

"Not really," Jeremy said. "But the cubs aren't going to be delivered until Friday of next week, so I thought maybe we could farm some of the cats out to foster families."

"Okay, make some calls to see if you can free up the space. If you can, call Fish and Game back to tell them we'll take them. We might even be able to get a few of the cats rehomed by Friday. Go through our files to see if there are any prescreened applicants who might be a good fit."

"I'm on it." Jeremy turned and left the office.

It always made me feel good when we were able to rescue an animal in need, but the truth was, we'd earned a reputation for being the ones to call when there was a need to find shelter for wild and domestic animals statewide. What we really needed to do was expand. I'd thought of talking to Zak about building a second shelter on the property. There was plenty of room to do so, but I kind of hated to start a second construction project when the first one wasn't completed yet. If all went well, the phase one construction for Zimmerman Academy should be finished by the first part of next year. While Zak's plans for the campus included several buildings, including the main building, where the classes were to be held, two large dorms, a separate library and gymnasium, and an administrator's residence, we planned to open in the fall of next year with only the classrooms and a single dorm ready. Phase two would begin the following year, including the second dorm and the library/gym.

Jeremy poked his head through the office door. "You have a call on line one."

"Okay, thanks," I said as I picked up the phone.

"Good morning, sunshine," Zak greeted me a bit too cheerfully.

"Please don't tell me you aren't going to make it home today."

"No, I'm coming home, but I'm going to be later than I initially planned."

"Is there a problem with your program?"

"No, that's up and running fine. But I spoke to Scooter's grandmother and he's ready to come home as well, so Alex and I are going to pick him up on the way."

I grinned. "That's great. I've really missed everyone."

"Yeah, it'll be nice to have the family back together. We're going to be pretty late by the time we make it all the way back to Ashton Falls, though, so no need to wait up. I'll try not to wake you when I get home."

"You'd better wake me. Just keep in mind that all the animals are sleeping in our room with me; it's the only safe haven from Twyla's kids, so don't trip on anyone when you come in."

Zak laughed. "I'll be prepared for the animal obstacle course. By the way, I spoke to my mother last night."

"She told me. She even apologized as instructed, so thank you for that."

"It's the least I could do. I wanted to...hang on; I have another call."

I waited while Zak put me on hold.

"It's Coop; I've gotta go. I'll see you tonight."

I knew the day was going to drag on endlessly if I didn't stay busy, so I did the assessment on the cubs set for release that I needed to turn in to Fish and Game and then helped Tiffany clean the dog runs before asking Jeremy if I could leave Charlie with him for a couple of hours.

I headed out to track down Ben Wild. It would be awesome if I could get this murder case wrapped up before my family returned home.

Ben owned a gas station at the edge of town. Most days between six a.m. and six p.m. that was where you'd find him. While he worked nearly every day, he did have the flexibility to come and go during that time, which he took advantage of by volunteering for community events and programs. I didn't think he could possibly have had anything to do with Edna's murder, but if Ben had been involved in Aspen's protest, maybe he had some insight into the dynamic of the group. After clearing Fritz, Jethro, Wanda, and Pete, I was back to thinking Edna's death might actually have been related to the cats after all.

"My argument with Edna in the post office had nothing to do with the cats," Ben said when I asked him about the incident. "She brought her car in here and authorized me to do over fifteen hundred dollars' worth of repairs and then told me she didn't have the money to pay me. Legally, I could have kept her car until the bill was paid, but she talked me into agreeing to a payment plan. After what happened with Fritz I should have known she never had any intention of paying me."

"When you said after what happened to Fritz were you referring to the fact that Edna fired him?"

"Edna didn't fire Fritz; he quit after she failed to pay him three months in a row. The only reason he hung in that long was because she kept telling him she was going to get some money from the neighbor over a property line dispute, but she never did."

"I thought that dispute came about because Edna had the property surveyed because she wanted to apply for a building permit. A woman planning to build a second barn doesn't sound like someone who's hard up for money."

"According to Fritz, Edna never planned to build a second barn. Somehow she found out about the well and had the property surveyed so she could force her neighbor to pay her for the use of the property where the well was located. I don't know all the details; I guess you can speak to Fritz directly."

"I heard he left town. Have you seen him?"

"No. Not for a week at least. If I run into him, I'll ask him to call you."

I left the gas station and planned to grab a sandwich. I parked my car in the alley behind the sub shop and was about to step out when I noticed something behind me that made me gasp.

"Where did you get that jacket?" I asked the filthy woman who'd been going through the Dumpster.

"I didn't steal it, if that's what you're thinking."

I reached out to touch the spot on the front of the jacket she was wearing, where a tassel was missing. "I didn't say you stole it, but someone definitely did."

"I found this in the Dumpster at the other end of the alley. If someone threw it out I figure I have every right to take it."

"When did you find it?"

"A few days ago. Does it matter?"

"Maybe." I reached into my pocket and took out the cash I had on hand. "I'll give you forty dollars for it."

The woman smiled a toothless grin. "I guess you got yourself a jacket."

I decided to take the jacket directly to Salinger. After having been in the Dumpster and worn by the homeless woman I doubted he'd be able to isolate any evidence that might have at one time been on it, but at least he had the tools to try. If the jacket didn't provide DNA or trace evidence that might help us, maybe I could find someone who'd seen the jacket discarded in the first place.

The Dumpster the woman indicated was the one where she'd found the jacket was clearly visible from both the far west corner of the park and the food truck that parked in the area during the summer months. I put the jacket in my car and grabbed the emergency cash I kept in my glove box, then headed toward the food truck.

"Can I help you?" the man, who wore a name tag that read *Hawk*, asked.

"A hot dog and a soda." I was pretty hungry because I'd never gotten around to getting that deli sandwich. "Were you parked here on Monday?"

"Every day this week. Gotta make a buck while I can. Once school is back in session the lunch crowd dries up. Mustard, onion, and pickle?"

"Yes, everything. I'm trying to find out who might have dumped a pink leather jacket in that Dumpster sometime in the past few days."

He frowned as he added the onion to my dog. "I do remember seeing someone with a pink jacket. The only reason I noticed it was because it's been hot this week, and it seemed odd that anyone would want to wear a jacket of any kind."

"I got it from a homeless woman I found going through the Dumpster down the alley. About yay high with no teeth." I held my hand up to a location just over my head.

"Yeah, I guess that's where I saw the pink jacket."

"And you don't remember seeing anyone actually putting it in the Dumpster?"

"Sorry." The man shook his head. "That'll be three-fifty."

I paid him and found a picnic table in the shade, contemplating the Dumpster while I ate my lunch. Edna's property was at least five miles outside town. There were dozens of Dumpsters in Ashton Falls. Why had whoever tossed the jacket placed it in this particular one? It wasn't in proximity to the murder scene, but perhaps it was close to something else. Perhaps the killer's home or business.

Still, if the killer had worn the jacket during the murder it would seem they would do a better job disposing of it. Salinger initially had thought Edna had pulled the tassel off the jacket during the struggle in which she'd died, but if someone had set out to frame Nona, perhaps they'd stolen the jacket, removed the tassel, and then dumped it while Edna was still alive. In terms of where the jacket had been dumped that made a lot more sense than a scenario in which the jacket was worn to the crime scene and then disposed of after Edna was dead.

The problem with this scenario was one of premeditation. If the tassel was brought to Edna's property and purposely placed in her hand after she died, that demonstrated intention and a well-thought-out plan. The fact that the murder weapon, the shovel, was simply tossed in the forest near the barn, was sloppy and spoke of a spontaneous act of violence brought on by rage or self-defense.

Something wasn't adding up.

I let my mind noodle on the possibilities as I slowly chewed my food. A carelessly abandoned murder weapon coupled with a carefully plotted frame-up didn't belong together in the same story. I tried to figure out one where the murder was unplanned but the frame-up was plotted. Suddenly, I knew exactly what could have happened.

"Okay, go over your theory again?" Salinger looked completely confused. I'd tried to walk him through my thought process, but apparently I hadn't communicated as clearly as I'd hoped.

"All right, but listen carefully this time. Person number one goes to the kitten mill for a reason having nothing to do with murder. While on the property an argument breaks out. Somehow Edna is hit with the shovel and dies. Perhaps the killer hit her out of rage, or even self-defense. When the killer realizes what they've done they panic. They toss the shovel into the forest and leave. At some point shortly after one of two things happens: Either the killer realizes they need to cover up what they've done so they go back to the property and place the tassel in Edna's hand, or they tell someone else what they've done and this other person orchestrates the frame."

Salinger drummed his fingers on the desk as he considered my theory. "For this to be true the person who came up with the frame would either have had to already had Nona's jacket or would have had to had access to it that afternoon."

"I suppose that does complicate things. Based on the timeline I've put together Nona would have been with Aspen when Edna died."

"Any chance Aspen is the killer and decided to frame Nona in order to save her own backside?"

I frowned. I didn't know Aspen all that well, but there was a discrepancy between her story and Nona's. It might be worth it to look into their whereabouts more carefully. If Aspen was the killer...

"I need to go," I informed Salinger.

"I thought you wanted to talk this through."

"I did. I mean, I do. But Zak and the kids are coming home early and I want to be home to greet them."

"Okay. Whatever you want. I'll talk to you tomorrow."

After I left Salinger's office I called Jeremy and asked him if he would drop Charlie off at the boathouse. I called Ellie to let her know Jeremy would be bringing him by and I would get him later. Then I headed toward the bar where I hoped to find Nona, who, in my opinion, had a lot of explaining to do.

Chapter 10

"Nona framed herself?" Ellie said later that afternoon.

"As odd as it sounds, she did. It seems Aspen went out to Edna's to talk to her about the sick kittens. She swears she only went to talk. She was going to offer to pay for them so Edna wouldn't destroy them. Edna told Aspen she'd rather kill them than let her have them and went out into the barn with the shovel intent on doing just that. Aspen grabbed the shovel in order to try to stop Edna from smashing the babies, and for some reason Edna let go, causing Aspen to fall forward and sort of spin around. Aspen still doesn't know what happened, but in the end Edna suffered a blow to the head. Aspen insists Edna was only knocked out and not dead after she accidentally hit her, but she panicked. She threw the shovel into the woods and went back to town, where she told Nona the whole sad story. Nona went out to the property on Aspen's behalf to make sure Edna had regained consciousness. When she realized Edna wasn't okay but dead, she came up with the idea of framing herself. She figured I'd get her off, and if Salinger was focused on her, he wouldn't be looking too hard at Aspen, who was a total mess by that point."

"Wow. That's some story. Did Salinger arrest Aspen?"

"For now. The attorney Zak hired for Nona is going to represent them both until they can get it all sorted out."

"Both?"

"Nona's guilty of covering up a murder, harboring a criminal, and interfering in a murder investigation. The attorney thinks in the end the district attorney won't want to go to trial and they'll be able to work out a plea bargain for both women."

"Okay, here's what I don't get: If Nona framed herself, why was she so mad about being arrested? She must have known she would be."

"She thought if she didn't demonstrate the proper amount of rage I'd know something was wrong right off. And she was right—I would have known. If Nona had done a better job of disposing of the jacket, I might never have figured this whole thing out."

"So Aspen's alibi about the staff meeting was a lie?"

I could see Ellie was still trying to piece the whole thing together. "No, she actually did have a staff meeting, giving her an alibi. Nona's the one who lied when she told me she was with Aspen until four. She was at Edna's, framing herself."

Ellie put her hand to her stomach. "Okay, so Nona went out to the property earlier in the morning and found the sick kittens. She then came back to Ashton Falls and told you about them. When you were unable to help she went to Aspen, who agreed to try to speak to Edna. They fought and Edna was hit with the shovel. Aspen panicked and came back into town, where she told Nona what happened. Aspen was a mess, so Nona volunteered to go out to the property to check on Edna, who was dead, so Nona came up with the idea of framing herself. At some point after Nona left Fritz came by with Tucker and they took the kittens, which they left on your porch. Shortly after that, the lady who had the appointment to purchase a kitten came by and found Edna dead."

"Exactly."

"That's crazy."

"Yeah, it really is. And tragic. Usually in a murder case there's a bad guy, but in this case everyone involved just wanted to save the kittens."

Ellie lifted her hand to her mouth.

"Are you still feeling sick?"

Ellie nodded and ran to the bathroom. Poor thing. Whatever nasty bug she'd picked up was really hanging on. She'd been sick ever since she'd been home from her visit to her mother. Maybe some fresh air would help. It was a beautiful day, so when she came back from the bathroom I suggested we sit out on the deck for a spell.

"It sure is a beautiful day," I started off once we were seated on the deck. "The lake is like glass. If Zak were going to be home earlier I'd suggest a boat ride under the moonlight."

"Just talking about a boat ride makes me want to puke."

"I'm so sorry you're still feeling so awful. Talk about a nasty bug. Did you go to the doctor?"

Ellie turned and looked at me. She didn't say a word, but the minute our eyes met she started to cry. I quickly set down my drink and ran to her side. I wrapped my arms around her as she sobbed.

"Oh my God. What is it? Did the doctor find something?"

Ellie didn't answer, but she did hug me tighter. I should have realized the minute I walked in the door that something was wrong. She'd done her best to follow along with my story, but she was distracted the entire time, asking me to repeat myself over and over again.

"Is it bad?"

Ellie nodded.

"Oh God, it's not something terminal?"

Ellie shook her head and pulled back just a bit. I handed her a tissue.

"I'm not going to die," she informed me. "It's not that."

"Then what?"

"I'm not sick, I'm pregnant."

This is the place in the conversation where even the seagulls in the background went totally silent. Ellie had been told by several doctors that she would most likely never be able to have children. This piece of news conflicted with everything I believed to be true and, I was sure, she believed true as well.

"Pregnant? Are you sure?"

Ellie nodded.

I had no idea what to say. Wow. Pregnant. Ellie wanted children of her own more than she wanted anything else in life. Was she happy? Was she terrified? Should I congratulate her or offer sympathy?

"How?" I finally settled on.

Ellie just laughed through the tears.

"I mean I know how, what I mean is," I paused as a new thought occurred to me, "who?"

Ellie started sobbing again.

I knew that Brady and Ellie were taking things slowly and as far as I knew they had settled into a comfortable friendship rather than a romance, but Ellie wasn't dating anyone else, so it had to be him. "Brady. It must be Brady."

Ellie shook her head but still didn't speak.

"Brady isn't the father?" I verified.

"Nooooo." Ellie was sobbing harder.

Okay, if Brady wasn't the father then who? "Maybe you should tell me what happened."

Ellie looked down at her lap. I could see she was struggling to regain control of her emotions.

"You know you can tell me anything," I encouraged.

"I know." Ellie blew her nose. She took a deep breath as she tried to quell her tears. "It's a long story."

"I'm listening."

Ellie looked so lost. No, not lost: terrified.

"What I have to tell you is complicated, so please just bear with me while I try to explain how something like this could have happened."

"Okay. You have my full attention." I leaned forward and placed one of my hands on her leg.

"You commented the other night that when you returned from Ireland you noticed Brady and I seemed to have made a connection," Ellie began. "You were right, we had. And over the next few months we became even closer. I knew he was still mourning the loss of his wife. He wasn't ready for a new relationship, and in the beginning I still had feelings for Levi, so I wasn't really after anything more than friendship either. The day before I left to visit my mother I spent the day with Brady and the kids. We had an amazing time together, playing at the beach, picnicking at the park, and feeding the birds along the lakeshore. After we put the kids to bed Brady offered me a glass of wine. I accepted and we spent a fantastic evening talking about anything and everything. It really was a magical time, and I felt closer to Brady than I ever had. Somehow, in spite of the fact that I never intended to have more than a single glass of wine, time got away from us, and before we knew it not only was it late but we had finished the entire bottle. Brady didn't think it was a good idea for me to drive, so he offered to sleep on the sofa so I could have his bed. I was happy and relaxed and the wine lowered my inhibitions."

"You slept with him."

"No, I kissed him."

"Kissed him? You can't get pregnant from a kiss."

"I know that. Let me finish. The kiss was just the beginning."

"Okay. I'm sorry; go on."

"When I kissed him he pushed me away and told me to stop. He looked like I had slapped him rather than kissed him. I was so embarrassed. I'd obviously been reading any signals I thought I was receiving from him wrong. I was both hurt and humiliated, so I grabbed my stuff and left."

Poor Ellie. To take a chance and put yourself out there like that only to be rejected. I could see why she'd taken off for an unplanned visit with her mother, but I still didn't see how she got from rejected to pregnant.

"And then…?" I encouraged.

"And then I did something incredibly stupid. I was confused and depressed and I needed someone to talk to. You were in Monterey with Zak, so I went to see Levi."

Uh-oh. I think I knew where this was going. I decided to help Ellie along and rip off the Band-Aid before she struggled too much trying to peel it off slowly. "You slept with Levi."

Ellie nodded. "He had already been asleep when I showed up at his door. He was dressed in boxers and was all groggy and disheveled. I couldn't help but remember how my kisses had affected him, which, given the circumstances, was a huge boost to my bruised ego. I started to cry and he pulled me into his arms to comfort me, and things progressed from there. It wasn't planned and it definitely wasn't wise, but the truth is, in spite of everything that's happened between us, we've always had fantastic chemistry between us."

"And after?"

"Afterward we both regretted it and agreed to forget the whole unfortunate incident. I love Levi. I'll always love Levi, but with all the starts and stops, we never could get fully on the same page."

Given the relationship Levi and Ellie have maintained since they were children, I could see how what happened could have happened; what I couldn't see was what was going to happen now.

"And Brady? It seemed like you planned to continue your friendship with him."

"I had decided to continue my relationship with Brady. I was so hurt and embarrassed at first, but when I got home from Levi's Brady called. He apologized for his reaction to what had happened and tried to explain the complicated emotions he was dealing with. I tried to understand, but I was dealing with complicated emotions of my own. I lied and told him my mom was sick and I needed to go take care of her. I assured him that things were fine between us and we could go back to the way things had been before that night." Ellie placed her hand on her stomach. "I guess things will never go back to the way they were before that night." She looked up at me. "What am I going to do?"

I took both of Ellie's hands in mine and I looked her in the eye. "You have to tell Levi."

"I can't."

"Can't isn't an option. He's going to be a father and he deserves to know what's going on."

Ellie started to cry again. "Levi has been very clear from day one that he doesn't want children. Ever. I can't let this baby ruin his life."

I took a deep breath. "I agree Levi may take this hard, but eventually he's going to notice that you're pregnant. I think it's best to tell him now. Who knows, maybe he'll actually be happy about it once he gets used to the idea."

Ellie's expression clearly communicated the fact that I was grasping at straws.

"Okay, maybe he won't be happy, but he loves you and he'll be there for you. Why don't you take a couple of days to get used to the idea before you tell him anything?"

Ellie looked somewhat relieved.

I placed my hands on Ellie's very flat stomach and smiled. "My God, El. You're going to have a baby."

Ellie started crying again, but this time I could see they were tears of joy.

We talked a while longer and then Ellie said she needed to get some rest. I promised not to tell anyone except Zak what was going on while she figured out how to deal with the situation. Poor Ellie had a long road ahead of her, but I was committed to do as I'd said and stand by her, whatever happened.

I returned to my car with Charlie. It was still early and I really didn't want to go home to join the Zimmerman clan. With everything that had happened that day, I felt wound up and in danger of a mental meltdown of my own. I was considering what to do when my phone rang. It was Salinger. He'd planned to talk to the district attorney; maybe he had news.

"Salinger."

"Donovan."

"Did you talk to the DA?"

"Yes."

"And...?"

"Edna Leech didn't die as a result of the blow to her head."

Chapter 11

I was so stunned as to be speechless. "Huh?"

"She was suffocated."

I frowned. "Suffocated? That makes no sense."

"I completely agree. This case has become a major pain in my backside. I have a whole passel of folks who are guilty of something, yet it appears that unless Nona or Aspen is lying, we still don't have the killer."

"Okay, this is crazy. Are you absolutely certain how Edna died?"

"Coroner said the official cause of death isn't the head injury, which I guess was minor, but suffocation, due, most likely, to someone holding something over her face."

Could this day get any crazier?

After I hung up with Salinger I decided to track down Nona. Chances were with the Zimmerman clan in residence she wasn't at home. I called her cell and found out she was in the bar where she liked to hang out. I told her I had news and would meet her in the coffee shop just down the street. I figured it would be too loud in the bar to talk.

When I explained to her what Salinger had told me, she was just as shocked as I was.

"I can understand how Aspen could have accidentally hit Edna with the shovel while trying to protect the kittens, but there's no way she suffocated her," Nona insisted.

"Are you sure? You've only known her for a short time. Accidentally hitting someone with a shovel is one thing, but suffocating a person implies intent."

Nona frowned. "What's going to happen now?"

"I'm not sure. Aspen is still in jail pending a plea bargain, but with this new information it might not be in the cards. And while I don't mean to alarm you, I wouldn't be a bit surprised if Salinger doesn't bring you in again as well. Someone smothered Edna with the intention of killing her. Based on the timeline, the two of you have to be his best suspects."

"Should I run?"

"I wouldn't. If you're innocent—and I assume you are—things will get straightened out." I looked at Nona with pity in my eyes. "You know that if Edna was dead when you arrived the odds are that Aspen is responsible for her death."

Nona didn't say anything, but I could see she was taking what I said seriously. She looked a lot older without the sass she usually displayed. My heart was breaking for her as she came to the same conclusion I had: Aspen mustn't be as innocent as she seemed.

I watched as the look on Nona's face went from defeated to determined. "No. Aspen didn't do this. I don't know who did, but I do know Aspen was truly traumatized when she accidentally hit Edna. Sure, she didn't handle it well, but she's just a kid. She panicked."

"A kid?"

"She's just twenty-two."

"Really? I thought she was older. She has a teaching degree."

"She graduated high school a year early and was on an accelerated program in college. What are we going to do? We have to help her."

I really had no idea. I supposed the first thing I needed to do was decide if I even believed in Aspen's innocence. This entire situation was bizarre. The traffic in and out of Edna's barn on the day she died resembled a freeway during rush hour. If someone other than Aspen or Nona actually killed Edna that would mean there was yet another person at play. The odds of that were astronomical. Unless...

"Okay, walk me through this again." I dug around in my backpack for a notepad and a pen. The timeline for the sequence of events was going to be tight. I wondered if another player was even a possibility.

"Ever since Aspen made me aware of the situation with Edna's cats I've been sneaking over to her place every now and then to take a peek and make sure the cats weren't in danger. Until Monday I hadn't seen anything that alarmed me enough to confront Edna, but the motherless kittens were in bad shape. I marched myself up to the door and demanded that they receive medical attention. Edna refused. That's when I came to see you. After I left your house I headed over to talk to Aspen. When she heard about the kittens she decided to take a stab at convincing Edna to do the right thing. Aspen tends to be a bit more diplomatic than I am, so it made sense that she be the one to speak to her."

"And what time would you say it was that Aspen left to go over to Edna's?"

"About noon."

"Okay, then what?"

"A short while later she came back, close to hysterical. When I calmed her down she explained that she and Edna had struggled, and somehow Edna ended up getting hit in the head. Aspen said she was alive but unconscious and she panicked. I decided to check out the situation myself. When I got there Edna was dead, so I took my jacket out of the storage compartment and framed myself. You know the rest."

"And the kittens were still there when you found Edna dead?"

"Yeah. I was going to wait a bit and then make an anonymous call reporting Edna's death, but the lady who came to purchase a kitten beat me to it."

"So Fritz and Tucker must have come by and taken the kittens after you were there. Do you have any idea what an incredibly small window of opportunity we're talking about? If someone smothered Edna after Aspen left and before you arrived, this person would have had to time it perfectly. There's really only one explanation."

"There is?"

"Whoever killed Edna was watching everyone come and go the entire time. When they realized Edna had been hit with the shovel they saw their opportunity to finish the job and took it. I suppose it's possible someone just happened by during the twenty-minute window between Aspen hitting Edna and you finding her dead, but it seems unlikely."

"I didn't see anyone else in the vicinity and Aspen didn't mention seeing anyone either."

"It had to be a neighbor. My money is on Jethro. What do you say we pay him a visit to check out our theory?"

"I'll drive."

I know I should have insisted on driving, but Nona had replaced her feelings of defeat with determination, and once she made up her mind about something there was no stopping her. At least I'd begun to get used to Nona's hell-on-wheels driving style and wasn't nearly as terrified as I had been the first time. Of course the biggest problem with taking Nona's hog was that it very loudly announced our arrival, leaving no chance for a surprise visit.

Nona parked in the drive in front of Edna's house. At least she'd realized that would give us a chance to scope things out before we actually knocked on Jethro's door. I climbed off the back of the bike and removed the helmet Nona had lent me. It was going to be several minutes at least before my legs felt really steady.

"What's the plan?" she asked.

Plan? I supposed it would have been a good idea to have come up with a plan before we made the death ride out to the county.

"I'll go have a chat with him. You wait here," Nona instructed.

"I can't let you go up to the door alone."

"Give me five minutes. If I'm not back call the sheriff."

Calling the sheriff suddenly sounded like a good idea. "Wait," I called after Nona as I dialed Salinger's cell.

Surprisingly, Nona stopped walking. I really hadn't expected her to. I was about to suggest that we just wait for Salinger to arrive when someone hit me on the arm from behind, knocking my phone to the ground. In the split second before I turned around I noticed Nona staring at someone from behind me.

It was Tilly, and she had a gun.

"It was you?" I breathed.

Tilly's face was twisted into a snarl that made her look like a demented lunatic rather than the sophisticated woman I'd met the other day. "You just couldn't leave well enough alone."

"But why?"

"Sometimes a woman has to fight for what's hers, but Edna didn't understand that. She thought she could have any man she wanted whether he was already betrothed to another or not."

"Betrothed?" I remembered Tilly making a comment about a wedding and a reception in her garden. "Donald," I realized. "You're Donald's fiancée."

"It was only a matter of time before she managed to get Donald under her spell, the way she did with Pete and countless others. I had to do it. Surely you can see I had no choice."

I'd been in pretty much this same situation a number of times before, so I knew agreeing with her was the best tactic, but apparently Nona hadn't had the same experiences.

"You always have a choice," Nona said. "Edna probably picked him 'cause he was sending her vibes. My guess is the poor victim thing was an act."

I groaned as Tilly lifted the gun and pointed it directly at Nona.

"She didn't mean it," I tried. "She's an old woman who doesn't understand about true love."

I glared at Nona in an attempt to communicate to her that it was time for her to let me do the talking. She glared back but, for once, remained silent.

"I've spoken to Donald," I continued. "I could tell his commitment to you was strong and true. Edna should never had tried to seduce a man who was so clearly in love with his fiancée. You're a very lucky woman and you'll make a beautiful bride."

Tilly smiled just a bit.

"No one needs to know about Edna, but if you use that gun now people are going to figure it out. How about we put it away?"

I was encouraged by the look of uncertainty on Tilly's face. At least she seemed to be thinking about what I was saying.

"I bet the dress you've picked out is lovely," I added as a means of keeping her attention on the wedding and not shooting us.

"It was my mother's."

"How very special. And your flowers?"

Tilly frowned. She didn't answer, but she did raise the gun just a bit. Dang, I was losing her.

"It's about time the cavalry arrived," Nona hollered, causing Tilly to look behind her, which allowed me to propel all one hundred pounds of my body at her, knocking her to the ground. The gun went off, Nona let out a very ungrandmotherly cuss word, and I hit Tilly with all my might, knocking her out cold.

I took a deep breath as I kicked the gun out of Tilly's reach. "Are you okay?" I asked the woman who stood behind me.

"I do believe the bitch has gone and shot me."

Chapter 12

I saw the blood on Nona's shirt and momentarily panicked. By this time Jethro had heard the ruckus and wandered over. I handed him the gun and told him to keep an eye on Tilly until Salinger arrived, and then I climbed onto Nona's hog and instructed her to climb on behind me. The dang bike weighed more than I did, but somehow I got us to the hospital without killing either one of us.

"Oh my God, I just heard." Ellie came running in through the double doors. "Is Nona okay?"

"I don't know." I was fighting the tears that were building up behind my eyelids. "I'm waiting to hear. How did you even know what happened?"

"Levi called me. He's here as well, parking the car."

"How did Levi find out?"

"Jethro called him. Not on purpose. You left your phone on the ground after you took off with Nona. You told Jethro to watch Tilly until Salinger got there, but your call hadn't gone through. He tried to use your phone to call Salinger, but he ended up pressing the wrong button. I'm

191

guessing Levi's number was in your call history. Anyway, when Levi heard what happened he called Salinger and then me. We figured you'd need reinforcements."

I hugged Ellie. "I do. I really do."

"Not a word to Levi about you-know-what."

"I won't," I promised as Levi rushed in and scooped me into his arms.

Waiting to find out how badly Nona was hurt was one of the hardest things I've ever had to do, in spite of the fact that I had my two best friends with me. I thought of calling Zak, but there was nothing he could do, and he'd just worry. I'd fill him in when he got home later that evening.

"How did you manage to get Nona to the hospital on that bike?" Levi asked.

"I have no idea. When I saw blood all over the front of Nona's shirt I panicked. Looking back, it was a stupid idea to bring her into town on the back of the bike. What if she had passed out and fallen off?" I was beginning to hyperventilate.

"But she didn't." Levi laced his fingers through mine and gave my hand a squeeze. "Jumping on the bike was the fastest way back into town. You probably saved her life."

"I could have used Jethro's old truck."

"Yeah," Levi admitted. "That might have been a better choice."

"What time is Zak supposed to be home?" Ellie asked.

"I'm not sure. Late. After midnight. I thought of calling him, but I don't want to worry him."

"Did you call to let the Zimmermans know what's going on?" Levi added.

"No, and I don't intend to. Not unless it looks like..." I couldn't finish the sentence. Nona couldn't die. In the short time I'd known her I'd come to love her. She just had to be okay. "What's taking so long?"

"It hasn't been that long," Levi reassured me. "Can I get you some coffee?"

"No. Coffee will only make me jittery, and I already feel like I'm going to jump out of my skin." I walked back and forth across the waiting room floor while Ellie and Levi watched me with looks of concern on their faces. I know how hard it can be when someone you love is in crisis and I didn't want them to worry about me, but as hard as I tried, I couldn't fake a nonchalant attitude.

"My buddy is letting me use his cabin in Vail this winter. I thought we could all go skiing," Levi suggested.

"Skiing?" Ellie commented. "Nona is in surgery and you want to talk about skiing?"

Levi shrugged. "I thought Zoe could use a distraction."

"I do need a distraction and I think it would be fun for all of us to go to Vail." Of course even as I said that, I realized Ellie wouldn't be doing any skiing this winter. "How big is this cabin?"

"Five bedrooms. It's really more of a house. I haven't been there before, but it looks awesome in the photos. There's even a giant hot tub on the back deck overlooking the mountains. I can picture us sharing a bottle of wine while we take a long soak at the end of the day."

Hot tubbing was another thing Ellie would be unable to participate in. Poor thing. Being pregnant was going to be a drag.

"It sounds wonderful," I said.

"I'll see if I can find out when the cabin is available," Levi offered. "I'll have time off around the holidays, so maybe we can do it then."

"Don't you think trying to cram a ski trip in with everything else that's going on over the holidays is sort of pushing it?" Ellie asked.

Levi shrugged. "Maybe, but it seemed worth bringing up."

"Mrs. Zimmerman," a doctor I'd never met before said as he came through the double doors that said "No Admittance."

"That's me." I stood up. "How is she?"

"She's lost a lot of blood, but she's going to be fine. Luckily, none of her vital organs were hit and you got her here in a timely manner."

I let out a deep breath. "Thank God. Can I see her?"

"She's in recovery and there's little chance she'll wake up until morning. I suggest you go home, get some sleep, and come back then."

It was decided that Levi would drive Nona's bike back to the house and I would go with Ellie. It was late and I was tired, but I was totally wound up, so I decided to head over to the boathouse to process a bit without having to deal with the Zimmerman clan. I knew that once my heart stopped beating a mile a minute I'd probably crash, so Levi agreed to come to Ellie's as well, and then drive me home when I was ready.

He frowned but didn't say anything when Ellie handed him a beer, me a glass of wine, and settled herself with a glass of water. I was sure he had no idea what was really going on, but he was perceptive, and he knew Ellie better than anyone on the planet. I had a feeling he was going to figure things out if she didn't share her news sooner rather than later.

"How was your doctor appointment?" Levi asked.

Ellie shrugged. "Fine. Just some female stuff."

"Female stuff?"

"Hormones," I pitched in. "Dang things get just a tiny bit out of whack and your entire body goes to hell."

"I see." It was clear he didn't see but decided not to push it.

"So how does the team look this year?" I asked. As head coach for the high school team, Levi was always up for talking football.

"Fine. Is there something going on that you girls are keeping from me?"

"Of course not," Ellie insisted. "Zoe is probably still in shock over what happened."

"Shock?"

"Nona could have died." Ellie must have noticed the real look of panic on my face because she added, "But of course she didn't and will be totally fine."

"The team looks good this year." Thankfully, Levi decided to play along with a game for which he clearly didn't know the rules. "We have a new running back who just transferred in from Bryton Lake. His addition to the team provides us with a double benefit because not only do we have his athletic ability but now Bryton Lake doesn't."

"That's great, Levi." I smiled as if this was the best and most important news I'd heard all day. He and I continued to talk football while Ellie was clearly struggling with runaway emotions. Once we'd exhausted the subject of football the conversation changed to the new school year and how it would affect Zimmerman Academy. After one glass of wine I claimed fatigue and asked Levi to drive me home.

"Is Ellie really okay?" Levi asked. He was clearly worried.

"She's fine," I assured him.

"And it's hormones that are making her feel so bad?"

"Yes," I responded honestly. "It is."

Levi took a minute to chew on that before he asked, "If something really was wrong you'd tell me?"

"Of course I would. Why would I keep anything from you?"

"I don't know. I do know that you and Ellie appear to have a bond that no longer seems to include me. I mean, I guess I get it. Things have been weird between Ellie and me ever since we broke up, and I imagine you've been put in a spot where you feel like you need to choose sides."

"I haven't chosen sides. I wouldn't. You and Ellie are *both* my best friends. I would never do anything to hurt either of you, but it's true that trying to play the middle can become awkward at times. Having said that, I promise you that Ellie is fine, though she may have something on her mind. If I were you, I'd wait for her to be ready to tell you what that something is."

Levi pulled up in front of my house. I could see he was struggling with the whole thing, and I guess I didn't blame him. If he and Ellie had a secret and I was the odd man out it would drive me nuts.

"I get what you're saying, but my instinct tells me Ellie is upset about something and it's my natural inclination to want to help her. In spite of everything that has happened I still love her. I'll always love her."

"I know." I placed my hand over Levi's. "If you want to help her just be there in a supportive, best friend way while giving her the space she needs to sort out whatever it is she needs to sort out."

Levi looked uncertain, but I could see he was willing to think about what I'd said.

I opened the car door. "I'll call you tomorrow after I see Nona."

"Okay. Thanks, Zoe. Have fun with your husband when he finally gets home."

"Oh, I intend to." I slammed the door and hurried up to the house. Ellie and Levi were both very important to me. I would be there for Ellie every step of the way, but I really hoped her pregnancy wouldn't permanently destroy our best friend triad.

Chapter 13

Saturday August 13

Zak was home. At least I hoped the delightful feeling of lips on my neck indicated that my very much missed husband was finally home. The room was dark, and although I couldn't see the man who was causing all sorts of delicious sensations to make their way through my body, I could feel the hunger in his touch. I wrapped my arms around his neck and pulled him toward me as his lips found mine. There were hundreds of things I should catch him up on, but when his hard body met mine I knew there was nothing so important that it couldn't wait a while longer.

It turned out that *while longer* never arrived. By the time we were both spent we drifted off to sleep, wrapped in each other's arms. Neither of us woke until the phone on the bedside table rang, disrupting our slumber.

"Hello," Zak answered tiredly.

He frowned as he listened. Then he turned and looked at me with a question clearly evident on his face. "Okay, thank you for the update." He hung up the phone. "Nona's in the hospital?"

"Yeah. I was going to tell you about it as soon as you got home, but one thing led to another and … Is she okay?"

"It sounds like it. That was the nurse. She said Nona was awake and driving everyone crazy, so I guess that means she's fine."

"Good." I let out a deep breath. "I was really worried. Can we see her?"

"Visiting hours start at one. I sort of hate to even ask because you look oh-so-good sitting there in nothing but a sheet, but don't you think you should tell me what happened?"

I filled Zak in on the murder investigation and the crazy turn of events I was still having a hard time wrapping my head around. I explained how Nona had been shot in the struggle but that the doctor had assured me nothing vital had been damaged. We agreed that we would go to see her as soon as visiting hours began. I was going to fill him in on the situation with Ellie, and Jeremy's engagement, but as his eyes turned from worried to sultry, talking was the last thing I wanted to do.

I crawled over across the bed and snuggled into Zak's arms so that my head was resting on his chest. I could feel his breath on my cheek as he wrapped his arms around me, releasing all the tension from my body.

"I've missed you." Zak kissed the top of my head.

"I've missed you too," I answered as I let my body melt into his.

"I'm sorry you had to deal with all this by yourself. First Nona and then my mother. It sounds like you've had a very difficult week and I hate that I wasn't here for you when you needed me the most."

"That's okay. It has been a really weird week, and your mother has been a challenge, but I know you would have been here if you could have."

"Is there anything else you need to tell me before we change the subject to what's really on my mind?"

I smiled as Zak made it very clear what was on his mind. "I've been thinking about a baby," I blurted out.

Zak pulled away slightly and turned so that he was looking directly at me. "A human baby?"

"Of course a human baby. What did you think I was talking about?"

"Knowing you? A puppy, a kitten, or possibly even a goat."

"Well, there is this kitten," I teased.

Zak adjusted his positon so that we were sitting up facing each other. "You've been thinking about *us* having a baby?"

I fought the momentary panic that quickly faded when I looked into Zak's eyes. "I have."

He reached out and took both my hands in his. "Are you talking about us having a baby *now*?"

I laughed. "Well, not right this second. I mean, these things take time. At least nine months. But if you're asking if I'm ready to start trying, maybe. I know I was mad at your mother for hiring a contractor to build a nursery without even talking to us about it, but I have to admit the idea of a nursery has caused me to think about things."

Zak frowned. My heart sank as he looked at me with an expression of doubt rather than excitement as I'd expected. "Are you ready for a baby?"

Zak tucked a lock of hair behind my ear in a slow, sensuous manner that caused a tingling sensation down my spine. "You know I am. I can't think of anything I want more than to see your belly swollen with my child, but I know you wanted to wait. If you're ready I am, but I want to be sure it's what you really want and this discussion isn't taking place because my mother pressured you into it."

"Have I ever let your mother pressure me into anything?"

"No, I guess not." Zak laughed. "So you really are ready to start trying?"

I put my hand on Zak's cheek and gazed into his eyes. "I am." I leaned forward and touched my lips to his before partially pulling away. "In fact, if you aren't busy, maybe we should start right now."

Zak smiled and pulled me into his arms. I wasn't sure how long it would take to plant the seed that would grow into the greatest expression of our love I could imagine, but deep in my heart I knew I was ready for this next phase of the Zak and Zoe story.

Whales and Tails Cozy Mystery:
Romeow and Juliet
The Mad Catter
Grimm's Furry Tail
Much Ado About Felines
Legend of Tabby Hollow
Cat of Christmas Past
A Tale of Two Tabbies
The Great Catsby – *July 2016*

Seacliff High Mystery:
The Secret
The Curse
The Relic
The Conspiracy
The Grudge

Sand and Sea Hawaiian Mystery:
Murder at Dolphin Bay
Murder at Sunrise Beach – *June 2016*

Road to Christmas Romance:
Road to Christmas Past

Kathi Daley lives with her husband, kids, grandkids, and Bernese mountain dogs in beautiful Lake Tahoe. When she isn't writing, she likes to read (preferably at the beach or by the fire), cook (preferably something with chocolate or cheese), and garden (planting and planning, not weeding). She also enjoys spending time on the water when she's not hiking, biking, or snowshoeing the miles of desolate trails surrounding her home.

Kathi uses the mountain setting in which she lives, along with the animals (wild and domestic) that share her home, as inspiration for her cozy mysteries.

Kathi is a top 100 mystery writer for Amazon and she won the 2014 award for both Best Cozy Mystery Author and Best Cozy Mystery Series.

She currently writes four series: Zoe Donovan Cozy Mysteries, Whales and Tails Island Mysteries, Sand and Sea Hawaiian Mysteries, and Seacliff High Teen Mysteries.

Stay up to date with her newsletter, *The Daley Weekly*
http://eepurl.com/NRPDf

Kathi Daley Blog: publishes each Friday
http://kathidaleyblog.com

Webpage www.kathidaley.com

Facebook at Kathi Daley Books -
www.facebook.com/kathidaleybooks

Kathi Daley Teen –
www.facebook.com/kathidaleyteen

Kathi Daley Books Group Page –
https://www.facebook.com/groups/
569578823146850/

E-mail - kathidaley@kathidaley.com

Goodreads:
https://www.goodreads.com/author/
show/7278377.Kathi_Daley

Twitter at Kathi Daley@kathidaley -
https://twitter.com/kathidaley

Amazon Author Page -
https://www.amazon.com/author/ka
thidaley

BookBub -
https://www.bookbub.com/authors/
kathi-daley

Pinterest -
http://www.pinterest.com/kathidale
y/